The quilt is proof that Walking Breeze is a Chelmsford. . . .

"This," she said and she held up the quilting, "was my mother's. From her time with the Shemanese. From when she lived here. In Mass-a-chus-etts."

My head was spinning. Thoughts crackled inside it like the fire in the hearth, making it hurt. Yes, I had a throbbing headache. And my face felt feverish. Perhaps I was coming down with something.

Fear. I was coming down with a good dose of the blue devils, as Mary would call it. One thought alone becalmed me.

I would get rid of this piece of quilting.

ALSO BY ANN RINALDI

The Quilt Trilogy: A Stitch in Time
In My Father's House
Wolf by the Ears

THE QUILT TRILOGY

Broken Days

ANN RINALDI

SCHOLASTIC INC.
New York Toronto London Auckland Sydney

ISBN 0-590-46054-4

12 11 10 9 8 7 6 5 4   9/9 0 1 2/0

Printed in the U.S.A.   01

To all my friends at the Crossing

Acknowledgments

I am indebted, first and foremost, to the marvelous history of this country, which is better, warts and all, than any story any writer could conceive. And thanks is due to those diligent souls who compiled the academic books I used, for they mined the gold and labeled it for me. Especially that wonderful Renaissance man of his time, William Bentley, D.D., Pastor of the East Church of Salem, Massachusetts, who faithfully kept a diary that brings alive the doings of Salem for so many years. For this novel I used Volume 4, 1811 through 1819.

Nearer to home, my appreciation goes to Marjorie D'Ascensio, Library Assistant II, Interlibrary Loan Department, Division of Adult Services, Somerset County Library, Bridgewater, New Jersey. Marjorie was tireless in renewing books for me, especially Bentley's diary, when I begged, "please, I've got to have it just a little longer."

Thanks go to Regina Griffin, my editor at Scholastic, for sharing my vision and allowing me to keep it intact.

I am, as always, beholden to my son Ron, who, as a teenager and young adult, got bitten by the history bug and passed on the disease to me. Ron and I, my husband Ron, and our daughter Marcella "attended the American Revolution" together in those wonderful years of the Bicentennial (from 1976 through 1983). As re-enactors we got flooded out in Sackett's Harbor, New York; we took part in the "Springfield death march," as we came to call the endless parade through North Jersey towns on the two hundredth anniversary of the Battle of Springfield; we were awakened at four-thirty in the morning by the military as we camped out on an airfield outside Savannah, Georgia, for the Siege of Savannah; we froze at Fort Lee, at Princeton; we heard the guns and the huzzahs of Yorktown, Virginia, in '81. And every Christmas I stand on the frozen ground and watch as Ron and my husband and a cast of hundreds cross the swollen waters of the Delaware with Washington.

How can you express appreciation for an influence that changed the course of your life? You can't. You hone in on specifics. So thanks, Ron, for sharing all those books with me from your extensive library on American and Military History. And for the memories.

THE QUILT TRILOGY

Broken Days

The Chelmsford Family

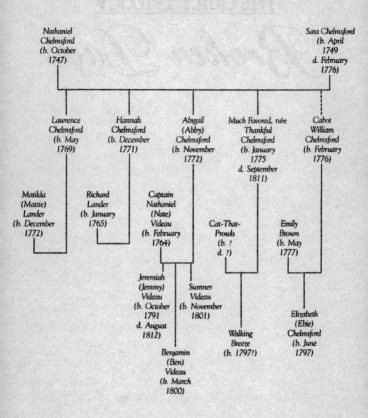

Chapter One

July 1811

Walking Breeze stood on the edge of a hillock counting the warriors on the riverbank. Twenty.

Only twenty were to accompany Tecumseh on this trip. They were gathered around the waiting canoes that were loaded with supplies and weapons.

In the center was Nay-tha-way-nah, also known as Cat Pouncing. He was Tecumseh's son. He saw her and waved. She waved back. But her heart felt about to burst with jealousy.

So, Cat Pouncing *was* going on this trip with his father. His bragging words had not been for nothing.

Well, if she were a boy, she would be going, too.

She and Cat Pouncing had grown up together. They had played and fished, gathered berries and hunted for small game. But now, though they were both fourteen, he was taller. His bronze shoulders had grown like an eagle's wings this summer. And he had started looking at her with a softness in his eyes, too.

Up until this summer there had been much *dah-quel-e-mah* between them. Family love. But now it seemed as if Cat Pouncing wanted to turn that love into *soos*. The love of a man for a woman.

Perhaps it was best he was going away, she thought. He has much growing up to do. He takes all his power from his father. His uncle, The Prophet, does that, too.

No, she thought, *I must wait and see what kind of man Cat Pouncing will become.*

Besides, if Cat Pouncing knew of the evil that was in The Prophet's one good eye when he looked at her, he would kill the man with a knife.

The Prophet was supposed to be a holy man. He carried sacred beads. He burned *nilu famu,* the sacred tobacco. He had visions.

But he had spied on Walking Breeze when she was in the river, bathing. Once he had tried to put his hands on her. Tecumseh did not know this about his brother. Not even Walking Breeze's mother knew this. She could tell no one.

The girl sighed. They had enough trouble in the village. Tecumseh could only take twenty men south with him. Because he must leave three hundred and fifty warriors to protect the village, lest the whites attack.

Ah, but last month, how different it had been! Then the great leader of the Kispokotha Shawnees had taken three hundred men, women, and children with him to Vincennes to meet the white chief, Harrison, who was governor of the Indiana territory.

She had gone on that trip, chosen by Tecumseh himself. Because her mother had taught her the white man's language.

She had seen the Shemanese General Harrison, who was buying up all the Indian lands. And his great *wigewa* with the thirteen chambers. She had heard him ask Tecumseh to turn over two Potawatomi warriors who had slain some white men.

Tecumseh had stood proud and refused, saying how, since the last peace was made, the general and his men had killed many Shawnees, Winnebagoes, and Delawares.

She had felt joy when Tecumseh told Harrison the land he purchased on the Wabash was their finest hunting ground. And whites should not try to settle on it.

The white general's face had become full of storm. "You are uniting all the Indian tribes into one nation!" he had accused Tecumseh, "to fight against us!"

"Did not the Thirteen Fires unite into one nation?" Tecumseh flung back at him. "Are they not seventeen fires now? Burning even brighter?"

Walking Breeze had heard Tecumseh say he would rather be a friend to the Seventeen Fires than to the British. What fools the Americans were, to keep taking lands from him.

She walked to her mother's *wigewa*, remembering how Tecumseh had taken her and her mother into his family after her own father, Cat-That-Prowls, had been killed in a battle years ago.

Thinking on it, she was filled with a bittersweet sadness. Not because Tecumseh was traveling south to try to get more tribes into his confederacy. Not even because the time it would take to accomplish this, the time of the broken days, would be nine moons.

She was sad because she knew she would never see Tecumseh again.

She was filled with the knowing of this. And she did not understand from whence it came. It was not a vision. She knew that. She was not holy enough. Besides, only men had visions, not women. But she accepted the knowing. She cleared a place inside her for the sadness it brought. She spread a blanket for the sadness. She gave it room.

She waited patiently outside her mother's *wigewa*. Tecumseh was inside. He had sent for her.

"Walking Breeze, come down to the river to see the weapons in my canoe." Cat Pouncing came up the slope.

"I must wait. Your father summons me."

He came to her. "How is your mother?"

"She is dying."

"I did not know it was so serious bad."

"Yes. Your father is saying goodbye. He knows

my mother will be dead before *pahcotai*, the season of autumn."

"I mourn for her. To me she was *neegah*."

Neegah. Mother.

"Come," Cat Pouncing said. "Say a proper goodbye. I will be gone many moons."

"I know. Nine."

He smiled. It had a grown-up sadness to it. "No. My father told Harrison nine because he knows Harrison will make war in his absence. But the time of the broken days is only four moons."

She stared into his face. "Is this true?"

"My father tells me everything. Come, say goodbye to me."

She allowed him to lead her a short distance away, under a tree. And in the farewell, she felt the sadness spreading its blanket further and further inside her.

For now came more knowing. That she would never see Cat Pouncing again, either. She became frightened. Did this mean he and his father would be killed on this mission?

How could she bear it? Then she saw Tecumseh come through the flap of her mother's *wigewa*. He stood, tall and strong and smiling at them. And Walking Breeze had another thought.

Perhaps it is I who will die.

She dropped Cat Pouncing's hand and went to Tecumseh. If *Moneto*, the Supreme Being, wants me to die instead of Tecumseh and Cat Pouncing,

I will do it gladly, she told herself.

"*Neeshematha,*" Tecumseh said. He called her little sister. He gestured that she should follow him. And he took her under the same tree where she'd stood with Cat Pouncing, who had gone back down the slope on a signal from his father.

"Your mother is very brave. As your father was when he took a musket ball meant for me."

Walking Breeze nodded, saying nothing.

"I wish you to care for your mother in my absence. I have told my sister, Star Watcher, that you should do this instead of helping to make bread and weave mats."

"Thank you." Walking Breeze wanted to cry. But she would not dishonor herself.

"The Prophet will be chief when I am gone. I have told the others. I do not wish to make him chief. I know his spirit is growing smaller and his need for power, larger. But he is my brother. People would see a weakness in my power if I did not trust him."

She felt his eyes burning into her. Did he sense the evil in The Prophet? Was that possible?

"I have told my sister and others to keep watch on him so he does nothing to break the peace. Harrison is looking for a reason to march on our village. All he needs is an excuse. *We must not give him that excuse.*"

Walking Breeze nodded, listening carefully.

"I have told my brother that if there is an attack,

he must not fight back. He is to move our people out. Listen to your mother. She hears much, even from her pallet. She has promised to be my ears while I am away. You must be her feet and lips. Do whatever she says to help keep the peace. Will you do this for me?"

"Yes. I will do anything to help."

He smiled and her heart raced. This man had worked for his people since he was a very young boy. He was gentle with women. He had never beaten his wife, though she had been lazy and had a scolding tongue and been a bad mother to Cat Pouncing. He had simply sent her away from him and finished the marriage.

He was modest, clean, kind, and just. He spoke the white man's tongue, could read the talking leaves, their books. His people trusted him.

He put his hand on her shoulder. "Your mother has always been one of us, though she came from the Shemanese. You are half-white, but you are all Shawnee."

She thought she would burst with pride.

"No matter what happens in the future, remember, you and your mother are big in my heart. You have given us much. Remember, too, that the Shawnee in you will keep you strong, forever."

Then he murmured *tanakia*. Farewell.

Tears burned her eyes, so she closed them. When she opened them again, he was gone. It was as if he had never stood there.

Only then did she let the tears fall. But she dried them quickly. It would not do to show her mother she had been crying.

It was September of that same year. In the morning sunlight, Walking Breeze dragged her feet, which were as heavy as her heart, through the colorful leaves.

She was on her way to The Prophet's medicine lodge. He had sent for her.

Yes, there had been peace since Tecumseh had left. Yes, Much Favored, her mother, was still alive, though she was growing weaker by the day.

But twice, The Prophet had tried to put his hands on Walking Breeze. Once he had come upon her when she was bringing water from the spring. But she'd run from him. Then he ordered her to his medicine lodge and offered her one of the many silver bracelets he wore on his fat wrists.

She had refused the bracelet. That had angered him. The porcupine quills on his moccasins shook as he stamped his feet.

"I am your chief!" he yelled. "You must obey me! Or I will punish you!"

"Tecumseh will kill you when I tell him this," she yelled back.

"Tecumseh will not believe evil of his brother!"

"He does already. He knows you refused the salt Harrison sent up the river last spring. And that you seized all the salt *this* spring, then told Harrison we hadn't gotten any for two years."

He threw things at her then. A pipe, a bear claw necklace, a bowl. Anything he could reach, he threw. But the words he threw were worse.

"You will not tell Tecumseh anything. Because you will not be here when he returns. I will be sure of this!"

That had happened one moon ago. Since then he had left her alone. But she sensed him watching her, waiting for a chance to punish her.

She had considered telling Star Watcher. But the woman was sulking in her *wigewa*, herself a victim of The Prophet's humiliating words.

The business with Star Watcher had started six suns ago. Seven young warriors had gotten permission from The Prophet to steal over to the nearest white village and take some horses.

The Prophet had said yes. There had been much loud talk when Star Watcher and her husband, Stands Firm, found out. Other braves also protested the decision.

The Prophet called them fools. "Can't you see? These young warriors are Shawnee, Kickapoo, Eel River, Wyandot, and Potawatomi. The tribes are working together. It is what Tecumseh wants."

More loud words. Star Watcher told her younger brother what trouble this stealing of horses would cause. And reminded him how they must keep the peace.

The Prophet screamed at her and sent her to her *wigewa*. She had not come out since.

Five suns ago, the warriors returned with the

stolen horses. Then yesterday, the white men had ridden into the village, demanding the horses back. The Prophet gave back the horses and told them the young warriors were just testing their strength. Then, when the whites rode off, he went into his lodge to have a vision. He did not come out all night.

This morning he summoned everyone in the village and said that in his vision he had learned that those horses belonged to the young warriors who had stolen them.

"Many warriors will now go and retrieve those horses," he said. "But no shots will be fired. For I am going to return to the white man something that was taken from him years ago."

Everyone wanted to know what that something was. The Prophet said they would know in time. They would see what a great chief he was.

And then, he had sent for Walking Breeze.

She stopped first at her mother's *wigewa*.

Much Favored scarcely sat up anymore. Half the time she was in a trance, speaking of her years with the Shemanese. She spoke about a sister named Han-nah, a brother, Law-rence, another brother named Ca-bot, and a father with red hair and one blue eye and one green one as she herself had.

She spoke of a place called Sa-lem, in the Shemanese land of Mass-a-chus-etts.

Now she raised her head. "Well, daughter?

Have you learned what The Prophet is returning to the white man?"

"Yes." Walking Breeze smiled, trying to be happy. "Me."

Her mother's eyes widened, then closed. Her frail chest heaved with the effort of breathing. "Did he tell you this?"

"No. But I am on my way to his lodge now. He has summoned me. I know it is what he will say."

"Why would he send you?" her mother asked.

"He doesn't like me. I think it is because I am half-white. He says no Shawnee should marry a white woman as my father married you. That our nation should be pure."

Her mother sighed. "If only Tecumseh was here."

"He told everyone that when he returns this possession to the white man, it will keep the peace, Mother. He knows he is wrong to have allowed the warriors to take the horses. But he cannot stop it now."

"So, Daughter," her mother said and smiled, "it is up to you to keep the peace then."

Walking Breeze felt as if she were dying, too. Her mother was agreeing to this.

"It has fallen to you to fix the damage this fool has done."

"I would do it with a glad heart, Mother," the girl said. "But how can I leave you?"

"It is I who am leaving you," her mother said.

Walking Breeze saw this was so. Sweat gleamed

on her mother's forehead. Her breathing was labored. She was in the grip of something terrible, that would not let her go. She looked into her mother's eyes. Both the blue eye and the green one had a glaze over them. Walking Breeze started to cry, softly.

"No tears, Daughter. There isn't time." Much Favored struggled to sit up. Walking Breeze helped her.

"You must do this for Tecumseh. He has done much for us. But first you must do something for me."

"Anything, Mother."

"Good. Go there in the corner, under my things, and fetch the piece of quilt."

Walking Breeze obeyed. She knew of the quilt. Her mother had it with her when she was taken, years ago. It had been a white woman's quilt then. Now part of it still had pieces of fabric from her mother's early life. But over the years her mother had added pieces of deerskin decorated with beads, a bit of fox fur here, some mink there, some bits of an Indian blanket, and other fragments of her new life.

The result, to Walking Breeze, was beautiful.

"You must take the quilt with you," her mother said.

Walking Breeze gave a cry of dismay. She knew how much the quilt meant to her mother.

"It will tell them who you are," her mother said.

Walking Breeze blinked. "Tell *who*, Mother?"

"My family," her mother said. "Back in Massachusetts."

Walking Breeze just stared at her. "Your *family*? You want me to go there?"

"Where else will you go when you are sent to the Shemanese?" her mother asked. "If you run away from them, you will be *matethi-i-thi* in any other Indian tribe."

Matethi-i-thi. Ugly. Walking Breeze knew her mother was right. But go to her *family*?

"How will I get there?" she asked, hoping to put briars in the path of her mother's thinking.

But her mother had already cleared the path. "Ask these white men to take you to Fort Wayne. There ask for Louis Gaudineer. You know of him."

Walking Breeze's head was spinning. There was a buzzing in her ears, as if the sun had lost its place in the heavens and the world was breaking into pieces inside her.

Yes, she knew of this Gau-din-eer, though she had never met him. He was a famous Indian agent who worked for the Seventeen Fires. He was big in her mother's heart.

Making all those words had wearied Much Favored. She lay back on her pallet. "Ask Louis to take you to my family in Massachusetts. He knows the way."

"But Mother!"

"I have prepared you. You know the language."

"But Mother, how can I leave you?"

"Just one thing." Her mother's voice was faltering. "The quilt . . . as fire to my family . . . smoke to Louis . . . tell him, instead that you are . . . my daughter. . . . We are good friends. . . . He is a good man. . . . He will take you on your word."

Then her mother's eyes closed.

Walking Breeze knew her mother's spirit was leaving her body. She waited. What had her mother said? That the quilt would be as smoke to Louis? Why? Because he had not known of its existence? Or because her mother wanted her to know that her word was enough to gain this man's favor.

So then, she would honor her mother. She would use only her mother's name to prove who she was with this Louis. It would take her far. All the way to Mass-a-chus-etts.

The waiting time was not long. Soon her mother's breath grew scarcer, then stopped.

Walking Breeze stayed. Her lamentations were quiet and brief. She did not want anyone to hear her. After a while she got up and gathered some things in a bundle. She put the quilt inside.

At the flap of the *wigewa* she turned to look once more at her mother, who seemed to be sleeping. She knew Star Watcher and Stands Firm would see to her now. No, she could not say goodbye to them. They might not let her go. And she must go.

She must keep the peace for Tecumseh.

• • • •

The Prophet leered at her with his one good eye. He looked like a jackal. He was so puffed up with his own importance, he would soon explode, like the white men's muskets.

"You will go with my warriors. You will be given back to the Shemanese, in exchange for the horses."

She stood straight and strong.

He was dressed in his ceremonial robes, but he did not look like a chief. Tecumseh never dressed like that. Tecumseh wore soft deerskin with bead-work.

This man was no chief. And he was no prophet. He was a fool. And someday Tecumseh would either have to kill him or disown him. Walking Breeze knew it was just a matter of time.

"You are worth nothing," he said. "You are trouble. I will tell Tecumseh that you are lazy and corrupt, that you did nothing but sit in the *wigewa* with your mother. Except when you came in here with your sly woman's ways, to tease me."

Walking Breeze knew Tecumseh would not believe this. But her heart broke into pieces knowing she would not be here when it was told to him.

"I shall remind my brother that your blood is impure. He will agree that I did the right thing sending you away."

She was careful not to make a sad face, for it would please him.

"Now you know what it is not to obey your chief. Now you know my power. Go. And if you do not obey my warriors, they have orders to kill you."

Outside, one of his warriors took her roughly by the arm. Walking Breeze's heart was so heavy she thought she was going to die. But she shook herself free and walked without need of him.

She walked as if she were only leaving for a morning's berry picking with Cat Pouncing.

Chapter Two

October 1811

I always thought it was strange the way Aunt Hannah called to tell us about the Indian girl just as Mary and I were about to go and look at those Indian paintings that morning.

It was more than strange. It was otherworldly. Mary said so. And Mary knows such things. She's my best friend, and I'm lucky to have her as a best friend. Because she has a sense about people that I don't.

Mary can see through people. And around them. And underneath them if she has to. That's when she's being ordinary.

When she's using her uncommon powers, she recognizes omens and isn't above giving a prediction or two. All in her regular everyday voice, using her regular everyday face. Nothing sinister. It's just like breathing to her. She doesn't call on the agency of invisible spirits, as Salem's seamen refer to their superstitions.

The day we heard about the Indian girl we were in the bedroom on the third floor. It was a holiday because there was a ship launching. And in Salem ship launchings are part of our religion. But Mary and I had seen enough of them to last a lifetime and were hiding out.

I, from Aunt Hannah, who wanted me to take a bundle to Georgie's house on Union Street. Mary, from her brother Moses, who captained for Silsbee, whose ship was being launched. So she was supposed to be at the launching.

"I'll go with you to deliver the bundle," she offered.

"If I deliver it, Mary, I'm going to make Georgie come out," I said.

"She hasn't been out in daylight in years. How are you going to do it?" Clearly Mary was taken with the idea. Georgie was a recluse. And part of my family.

"I'll leave the bundle at the edge of the walk. She'll have to come out. Or starve."

"She'll starve. And you'll be to blame for it."

"I don't care. I'm tired of being teased at school because she's part witch."

"She's not part witch."

"Then why do they put a sign on her front door every time somebody's cow dies or a man falls from a ship's rigging?"

"Because Georgie is the closest thing to a witch we've got in Salem. The real reason people hate her is because she's part Indian."

Well, I knew that. "It's all Aunt Hannah's fault," I said. "If she hadn't let her go west years

—— 18 ——

ago, she wouldn't be daft. She stayed near a year. And came back more Indian than white."

"Then why did your aunt let her go?"

"Because Uncle Louis wanted to see his daughter. He was an Indian agent by then. And when Tecumseh came to make treaties with Uncle Louis, she met him. I don't think she ever got over that. She talks about him now, all the time, him and his one-eyed brother. She even tried to follow him back to his village one day. Uncle Louis had to go fetch her."

"What happened?" Mary was wide-eyed.

"I'm not supposed to talk about this outside the family," I said.

"You said I'm closer than the family."

That was true. "Georgie kept trying to run away and find Tecumseh's village. Uncle Louis sent her home."

"And she came home daft?"

"No, but she wasn't the same. I was five when she left. She was thirteen. She used to read to me and take me places. When she came back she wouldn't pay me mind anymore."

"Is that why you don't like her?" Mary asked.

"If I don't like her it's because of the grief she gives the family," I said.

But Mary was too smart for that. "I think you will never forgive Georgie for being different when she came back," she said.

I shrugged. "She wouldn't have anything to do with any of us. She wore Indian clothing and wouldn't go to church. She wanted us to call her by her Indian name. Night Song. Aunt Hannah sent her to Cummington, to her friend, Sarah Bryant, to learn about fabrics. She ran away. No girl has ever run away from Sarah Bryant. Aunt Hannah was mortified."

"Where did she go?"

"West. She attached herself to a wagon train. Grandfather had people looking for her. They found her at Pittsburgh."

"How exciting!" Mary's eyes were bright, as with fever. "I think your family is so exciting, Ebie."

I lay on my back on the Persian carpet, staring up at the widow's walk. "No one's been able to do anything with Georgie since. Grandfather gave her the house on Union Street, to get her out of the way. But all she's done is make trouble."

Mary sat on a nearby chair, ruminating. "Why did Aunt Hannah take her back?"

"Guilt," I said.

"But none of it was her fault."

"You don't understand this family, Mary. They're all belabored with guilt because my aunt Thankful was taken by Indians years ago. It's ruined them all. Anything to do with Indians just benumbs them. Aunt Hannah's been trying ever since to make up for it with Georgie. That's why she abided it for two years after she came back. But I don't have to."

My breath was spent. "I wish this room was mine," I sighed, giving the conversation a new turn.

"Have you asked your aunt for it?"

"A million times. No, she says, it's Aunt Abigail's. And when she returns to Salem, the room must be ready for her." I sat up, abruptly. "Do you know that for twenty-three years this room has stood ready for her? She's never come back since the night she eloped from the widow's walk. Sometimes I get so tired of my family, Mary. They're all strange."

"No stranger than mine."

Mary's parents were old. Her father had taken part in the Boston Tea Party in '73. He was sixty now. So was her mother. They doddered about.

She had four older brothers, all seamen. I would have killed for one brother. I had cousins down south. They were the children of Aunt Abigail. One of them, Jemmy, wrote to Aunt Hannah all the time. Always he promised to come and visit. But so far he hadn't.

One of Mary's brothers always tried to be home while the others were at sea. But if it was Moses, as it was now, life could be difficult. Moses saw no difference between their house on Derby Street and the East Indiaman he captained. He didn't want his pronouncements questioned.

Mary questioned them constantly. It made for lively discourse in their house.

"Speaking of Indians, you promised to show me the paintings you found last week, Ebie."

I had. "All right, come on."

The paintings were half-hidden behind an old sailor's chest. And when I'd found them, they'd befuddled me.

It isn't difficult to befuddle me. I live in a state of befuddlement, it seems. My family does it to me, because there are so many things they won't speak of in my presence.

One of those things is the trip west that Grandfather took with Uncle Lawrence and Aunt Thankful years ago.

It was the trip on which Aunt Thankful was taken by Indians.

I knew Uncle Lawrence hated Indians. Now here were these pictures he'd painted. All of Indian chiefs.

The pictures were beautiful. The chiefs were resplendent though they wore only leggings and their faces and chests were painted. Their lances had strips of ermine on them. They had long braids.

Uncle Lawrence did these. Uncle Lawrence who, when the time comes, will use his militia to crush the Indians who are aligning themselves with the British, I thought.

It made no sense. But then so little about my family did.

I told no one but Mary of my discovery. But I

found myself looking at Uncle Lawrence a little differently.

The only way I survived was by understanding the foibles of my elders. Aunt Mattie and Uncle Lawrence had never been blessed with children, for instance. That gave them a whole set of foibles all their own.

Still, I had always considered them the ones not given to lunacy in the family. Now, finding out I was likely wrong about Uncle Lawrence did nothing to help.

"You just promise," I cautioned Mary, "not to tell anyone about these paintings."

"Did I tell anyone that Benjamin Cleveland took you to the Crowninshields' stone lookout tower on Winter Island on the Fourth of July and kissed you?"

"We were watching an East Indiaman stream out of the harbor. And we were looking for the sea serpent. Benjamin loves ships. His uncle was sending him to work in his Boston countinghouse. And Benjamin is going to war when it comes, so he can get experience and become a merchant. That's why I kissed him."

"Is war coming, Ebie? I can't ask in my house. Moses says war is bad for trade."

"It's coming," I said. "Uncle Lawrence hasn't made his militia the best in the country for nothing."

For some reason, that beset Mary. And we stood

for a moment, taking each other's measure.

We were the same age, fourteen. In looks and behavior we were opposites. Mary had fair hair, a round face, and blue eyes. But she worried she was too "sturdy." She was sturdy, but she was pretty, too.

I was thin, all angles. My dark hair was curly and unruly. My eyes brown and too large. My bosom not nearly as respectable as Mary's. Sometimes I thought I was pretty, but I couldn't be sure.

Nobody in the family ever told me I was pretty. You need to hear that kind of thing from your elders. Once they'd mentioned that I looked like my mother. That fact alone seemed to make the matter off limits for discussion.

"Oh, Ebie," Mary whispered, "if there's war, what of my brothers?"

"Your brothers will be fine."

"Why don't I feel that?"

"Because you can see answers to everyone's problems, but not your own. Anyone who can go to sea has the mettle for war. Uncle Lawrence said so. Now what do you think of the paintings?"

She touched them. "I think your uncle Lawrence was once inordinately fond of the Indians."

"He hates Indians."

"He loved them once. You can see that here. He doesn't paint anymore, does he?"

"No."

"After the Indians betrayed him, he couldn't paint anymore. Don't you see?"

"Aunt Mattie is always after him to paint. She says he has the gift."

Mary was silent for a moment. "I think they're poetic," she said.

"The paintings?"

"No. Your family. They're all very poetic. Even Georgie. Look how she's welcome in the most proper houses, because she's a sin eater. That's a forgotten New England custom, Ebie. And she's brought it back."

Georgie went into people's houses at night and prayed over their dead at wakes. To take the sin from them. People paid her for this. It mortified my family, who considered it on the same level as what Catholic priests did. And priests were papist fanatics.

"And look at your uncle Louis. Don't you think it's poetic that he's an Indian agent and can't help his own daughter?"

Only Mary would see the poetry in that.

"And you call him Uncle Louis when he isn't your real uncle. And you have an uncle Richard, who isn't real, either. And both are in love with your aunt Hannah, the spinster. Oh, Ebie, your family is *so* poetic!"

"Aunt Hannah is no spinster, Mary. Not in word or deed."

Her blue eyes widened in delight. "What do you know? Tell me!"

"I sneaked a look in her journal. But I can't tell you. It isn't my secret to tell."

"Tell me," she insisted.

But I wouldn't. I have learned it is important to keep some secrets. And let them go at certain moments, when you need people to pay mind to you. Besides, I think Mary respected me for not telling. She stopped pushing.

"I'm going to see to it that Richard Lander becomes my real uncle," I told her. "I'm looking after his interest with Aunt Hannah."

"They've been betrothed *twenty-three* years, Ebie. Who stays betrothed that long and never marries?"

I took up for Uncle Richard then. "He's always been out of the country. Privateering, or being taken prisoner. Once by Malays, once by Barbary pirates, and now by the British. That takes a toll on a man, Mary."

She nodded, transported by the romance of it. "Suppose your father can't secure his freedom over in England?"

"My father knows a man in Parliament who can."

We sat in silence for a moment. "Do you think your aunt Hannah still loves your uncle Louis, Ebie? Just a little bit?"

I knew she did, from the journal. But I couldn't tell. "She says they are old friends who turn to each other in times of trouble."

"I'm never giving my heart to a man," Mary said. "Love isn't worth the bother, Ebie. Look what trouble it's caused in your family."

As I saw it, lack of love caused the trouble in my family. But I didn't say that. "I intend to be like Aunt Hannah. And have two dashing men in love with me." That's what I did say.

Mary smiled, as if she were years older and wiser. "Likely you will." She said it as if she was privy to something.

Before I could ask, Aunt Hannah's voice came from below stairs, then. "Ebie! Come down this minute! I have something to tell you."

We went downstairs, past landings with Persian carpets, windows draped with damask curtains, ancestors staring at us from gold-framed paintings. The house was full of elegant trappings brought by Uncle Richard from all over the world.

Aunt Hannah had a letter in hand. She was wearing her green silk. This was her daughter-of-a-prominent-merchant-family dress. Crimson was her languishing heartsick maiden's dress. She wore brown when she was long-suffering and blue when she taught the children who worked in Grandfather's mill.

You didn't shilly-shally with her when she wore dark blue. I was glad she was not my teacher. Mary and I attended Mrs. Peabody's school. Mrs. Peabody wore only gray and was as dull as yesterday's squash. But at least you could always count on what mood she would be in.

Nevertheless, my whole being was put on notice in Aunt Hannah's presence. She was thirty-nine, well past a woman's prime. But her beauty always startled me. It wasn't *decent* for a woman to be so beautiful at thirty-nine. Was it?

"I've a letter from Uncle Louis! He's coming for a visit."

I knew what Mary was thinking, that we'd summoned Uncle Louis with our talk. It *was* eerie.

"Ebie, do you know of my sister, Thankful?"

How could I not? "Yes, ma'am. She had red hair, one blue eye and one green one. She was Grandfather's favorite."

"Well, it seems she's been alive all these years! Fancy that!"

I didn't want to fancy it. Not at all.

"Louis writes she just died last month. And he is bringing a young girl home with him. An Indian girl who knew her."

Mary touched my hand. Again I knew her thoughts. *Didn't he befuddle things up enough? Now he's sending another Indian girl? What's wrong with you people?*

"Half-Indian," Aunt Hannah amended, as if that cleared everything up.

Georgie was half-Indian.

"Louis writes that he doesn't want to get our hopes up, but he thinks she is Thankful's daughter."

The watch went by outside, calling, "Eleven bells, clear weather, and all's well." His voice faded. Mary and I stared at each other. And I knew that all was not well. And that all would probably never be well again.

Aunt Hannah went a little daft then. She yelled for Cecie, our housekeeper, to go and air out Aunt Abby's room. She clutched the letter to her breast. "Oh, I always thought it would be your aunt Abigail's boy who would come to visit us! And now it could be Aunt Thankful's girl! Oh, Louis could appear at any moment! What will he think of the house on Union Street! I must get it cleaned up. Ebie, go deliver that bundle. But don't tell Georgie her father is coming. Not yet." And she ran into the kitchen.

Mary and I looked at each other. "Trouble," Mary said.

"She's giving this girl Aunt Abby's room," was all I could say.

"Never mind the *room*, Ebie. If she's Thankful's daughter, she's your *cousin*. You've got a half-Indian cousin."

We sat down on the bottom step. "My father won't like it," I said.

"He isn't *here*, Ebie. Why bring him into it?"

"Because he's all I can think of. You know how he has no esteem?"

Mary shook her head, yes, but I could tell she didn't know. Mary had enough esteem for six people. When you're like that you don't know what it's like for a grown man not to have any.

"He's got no esteem because of how my grandfather always treated him."

"If he's got no esteem, it's because your mother left him, Ebie. Men get that way when their wives run off."

"Grandfather never treated him like a son. If he had, Mother wouldn't have had to run off."

"Don't cry," Mary said. "Why are you crying?"

"You wouldn't understand."

"I do understand. Can I talk plain?"

I nodded.

"You're afraid your grandfather will lose his wits completely if this girl is Thankful's daughter. Because he only just started to pay mind to you after all these years. He's promised to take you to England when you're sixteen. And that made your father so happy, it made up for the things your grandfather didn't do for him."

I just stared at her. "You have uncommon powers, Mary, truly."

"It's a grave responsibility," she said. "I don't think you should worry so about your father, Ebie. He's doing fine."

"I have to. Aunt Hannah said there are a lot of women in town who are smitten with him. But he doesn't think himself worthy. He has no esteem."

"You'll go to England, Ebie. All the leading merchants take their children or grandchildren. It's a matter of prestige."

"I don't care a pig's ear about England, Mary,"

I said fervently. "But I do care about my father. You're right. I have my place as the only grandchild Grandfather will acknowledge in this family. And I won't give it up to any stupid Indian girl who walks in here and lays claim to it."

She gave me her handkerchief. I wiped my face. She stood up. "What will you do?" she asked.

"I don't know. But I'll do something. Come on, let's get this bundle to Georgie's. I'm just mad enough to make her come out this morning. It'll be good practice."

Chapter Three

Mary and I walked past Georgie's house every day on the way to school. So did many of our schoolmates. Not a day went by that they didn't taunt me about Georgie.

"Witch, witch, come out, witch," the girls would yell as they ran by Twenty-one Union Street. They always ran by. To walk was surely to tempt the agency of invisible spirits.

They said the house was haunted.

I didn't hold with spirits. But for me that shabby little house, with its sagging steps, its shutters half-hanging off, and its weed-choked yard, was haunted for another reason.

I was born in that house. My grandfather gave it to my parents after they married. It was the only thing he ever gave them, and I think it must have killed him to do it.

My father could afford no dwelling place of his own then. He would not live on my mother's marriage portion. He was working for Uncle Richard, yes, but some of their ships were captured by the French who were turning privateers loose on American shipping.

The British had been stealing our ships for years. But then along came Mr. Jay with his treaty and so America and Great Britain settled their differences. The French were plagued because of that treaty. So then they started in jumping our ships. I know all about it. Uncle Richard told me. "It's like when you fight with Mary," he said to me. "Then somebody else starts to make friends with her and you get all jealous. You may be angry with her, but you don't want anybody else being friends, either."

So because the French were jumping all over our ships, insurance rates went up. Especially for voyages to the West Indies. From six percent in 1796 to thirty percent in 1798, Uncle Richard said.

I was born in 1797. My father had no money.

There they were at Twenty-one Union Street, my parents. And Mama was making the sad little house like a castle. She had a flower and vegetable garden. She put a highpost bed in the bedroom, Hepplewhite table and chairs in the dining room, and Venetian carpets in the parlor.

When I was a year old, my father was on a voyage for Uncle Richard. The West Indies. This was supposed to be a short hop, only three weeks to get home once he was there. But then my father found out he could sell his cargo in Naples for three times its original cost, so he weighed anchor and went to Naples.

Even with a good prevailing westerly wind, that takes five or six weeks. Then home again to America.

Mama left when he didn't come home in the expected time. She thought he'd been lost at sea or taken by pirates. She was tired of living alone. She left the Hepplewhite table and chairs, the Venetian carpets, and the highpost bed and went home to her father in Rhode Island. No amount of talk from Uncle Richard or Aunt Mattie could stop her. God couldn't have stopped her if he appeared in the vegetable garden in a burning bush.

When my father came home he was madder than if Barbary pirates had jumped his ship, which they weren't above doing when they got the chance. He went to Rhode Island, fetched me home, and put me with Aunt Hannah. The house on Twenty-one Union Street stayed empty a number of years, till Georgie moved in.

Georgie got the Hepplewhite table and chairs, the Venetian carpets, and the highpost bed. I hated her for that. I had nothing from my mother, not one thing I could hold in my hand that had been hers.

And every time I step inside the door to deliver a bundle to Georgie, I look around. I try to find some evidence of my mother in that house. But the years and the dirt and gloom have turned whatever remains of her into disrepair.

For years my mother was as one dead to us. My father put her aside. He divorced her. To make mention of her causes him pain. So I never do it.

One day one of my schoolmates threw a stone and broke a window of the house. I cried. Mary was hard put to stop me. It seemed so wrong that anyone should visit destruction on the already sad place where I was born.

That was the morning we met the Hathorne boy.

He was peering at us over the back fence. He lived in the house behind Twenty-one Union Street. He came through a hole in the fence and stood in the yard, watching me cry.

"Go away, Nathaniel," Mary said.

"You oughtn't to cry," he said. "Georgie doesn't cry when they throw things at her."

I wiped my face. "Do you know her?"

He nodded solemnly. He was about seven and had a head full of chestnut curls and large, sad eyes. "Yes. She only comes out at night. People throw things at her if she comes out during the day. She told me."

"She talks to you?" Mary asked.

"Yes. She's a recluse, like my mother. *She* hasn't come out of her room since my father was lost at sea three years ago."

"Nathaniel's ancestor was a judge in the witch trials," Mary said. "One of the women he condemned put a curse on him and his children."

"And his children's children," Nathaniel said. "That's me. I have the spell of witches on me. That's why Georgie likes me."

I felt a kinship with the beautiful little boy. From one of my bundles, I gave him a sweet. And I never cried again passing Twenty-one Union Street. If Nathaniel could be brave, with a father lost at sea and a mother who was a recluse, so could I.

But when we got to the front gate that morning, I discovered that being brave was a matter of degree. And for the moment I wavered. Mary and I just stood there looking at the desolate yard. Then I saw a movement behind one of the windows.

"Someone's in there with her," Mary said. "A sailor, most likely. My brother Moses says sailors visit her all the time."

"I'm leaving the bundle," I said. And I left it.

We walked away. "I'm sick and tired of how she brings disgrace down on us, Mary. And worse than anything, she gets forgiven by the family all the time. And my mother isn't. Did she ever consort with sailors, like a doxie? No, all she did was go home to her father. Because she was tired of living alone."

I started to run. And to cry.

It was Mary's considered opinion that dogs would get the food bundle that night. Dogs didn't get it. Boys did.

Salem had a problem with warring groups of boys. The up-in-towners were always fighting with the downtowners. In winter they threw iced snowballs at each other. In summer, stones and bricks. Many times innocent people got caught in the middle. But there was nothing the town fathers could do to stop them.

That night they made ill usage of Georgie's food. They threw it all over the ragged front yard. The butter and eggs were dashed against the front of the house. Eggshells lay all over, as did pieces from the broken butter crock. Great globs of cheese were strewn about. So was the gingerbread.

But it was what they did with the uncooked chicken that had everyone distraught. They went absolutely daft with that.

They hung it from a small pear tree in the front yard. A sign was strung around its neck. The sign read: This is what Salem does to its witches.

Chapter Four

The town fathers were not amused.

"They're near to distraction," Parson Bentley said.

He was at the breakfast table next morning with Aunt Hannah. They were old friends.

"You know how touchy the town fathers are about any reference to the witch trials," he was saying. "It's in their best interest not to raise such a specter. They want Salem thought of as a God-fearing town."

"Mary's brothers say there are brawls every night in the taverns." I couldn't help saying it. There were all kinds of sailors in Salem all the time. They didn't act as if they feared God. And as far as I could see, the regular people didn't, either.

"That is not our concern," Aunt Hannah said. "What happens at Georgie's house is. And if you'd brought the food inside, Elizabeth, this wouldn't have happened."

"Am I to blame for what those boys did?"

"We must accept blame," Aunt Hannah said.

She used her schoolmistress's voice saying it. When she said "we" that way, I just knew she considered herself far above the whole business.

"Out of respect for your grandfather, the town fathers will refrain from taking any action about last night," Parson Bentley was saying. "They ask only that someone clean up the place."

"I've sent for Lawrence," Aunt Hannah said. But she looked at me. "He will take charge. Excuse me, Parson, I must prepare my lessons. Elizabeth, I think Parson Bentley has some thoughts he wants to impart to you." And she left the room.

I understood then. The parson was here on official business. He'd come for the town fathers and Aunt Hannah had recruited him to bawl me out.

I felt sorry for him. He stood as she took her leave. He was a cheerful, balding man with nice hands. I liked him because his sermons weren't filled with dire predictions of hellfire. And he didn't preach against the impurity of women, like so many other preachers in Salem did.

He knew Arabic and French. He was friends with Thomas Jefferson and Paul Revere. His father had rowed Paul Revere across the Charles River the night of Revere's famous ride.

But he knew young people better. He was always planning outings for them. I often thought he was happier doing that, and fussing with his collection of rare curiosities brought to him from around the world by ships' captains, than preaching and bawling people out.

"Your aunt is in a state of anxiety since she received that letter from your uncle Louis," he said.

"Am I at fault for what those boys did?"

"I am sure if you knew what would happen, you wouldn't have left out the food, would you, Ebie?"

"No, sir. But Aunt Hannah always wants Georgie to come out. And she'll never come out if we keep bringing her things."

"Is that the real reason you left it?"

"Georgie can do anything she wants to disgrace this family and be forgiven. And they'll never forgive my mother."

"Ah, so that's the reason then," he said. He nodded, as if he understood. And it came to me that likely he did. That he'd known everyone in my family for years. He knew things about them I could only speculate. But he couldn't tell. Because being a parson meant he had to take people's secrets to the grave with him.

I wondered how he kept all those secrets inside him without bursting. I figured that was why he wore his long black robe with the wide sleeves. It covered all the places he was bursting with people's secrets, dying to get out.

"They expected more from your mother, Ebie," he said. "And from you. As they do from me."

"Well, it isn't fair."

"No, it isn't. When you're good, people expect you to go right on being good. And not have one bad day."

"Parson, can I tell you something?" I asked.

"Certainly, Ebie."

"I'm not good. Not really."

He smiled. "Neither am I, Ebie. But people see us that way. So we mustn't disappoint them. It's a terrible burden."

He smiled and sipped his coffee. And I got this feeling that there was some other matter he wanted to discuss with me, that this was all a prelude to something.

"Parson, you've known my family a long time, haven't you?"

"A very long time, Ebie."

"This half-Indian girl Uncle Louis is bringing home. What do you think of her?"

I sat on my bed in my room. Aunt Hannah had gone to the mill. The parson was still downstairs. He'd promised to wait for Uncle Lawrence and smooth things over for me.

In return, I had entered into an agreement with him to be nice to the girl Uncle Louis was bringing. I could scarce believe that I had done it.

But it had happened in a moment of weakness. I went over my conversation with the parson in my head.

"I'm sure she's young and frightened," he'd said of the half-Indian girl. "I hear from Hannah she is quite pretty and speaks English." He was working on me to be nice to her.

I didn't care if she spoke Greek. And I told him

so. "She'll worm herself into Grandfather's affections. Just because she's Aunt Thankful's daughter."

"Your grandfather loves you, Ebie," he said.

I hate it when grown-ups do that, try to wash things over with words that don't mean anything. I was disappointed in the parson and told him so.

"You said you would always speak the truth to me," I said. "My grandfather doesn't love anybody, except Aunt Thankful. You know that."

He felt ashamed. "I'm sorry, Ebie, you are right to chide me. And you are right about your grandfather."

"I don't care for myself, Parson. It's for my father." Then I told him how so many women were smitten with my father. And he needed his esteem.

He listened. Then he prayed with me, right there at the Chippendale table. He prayed that my grandfather would take me to his heart when he returned. And that I would find it in my heart to be kind to the half-Indian girl. I still hadn't promised that I would be.

It was the sea serpent that did it.

He promised, when he finished praying, to take me with him to see the sea serpent. "It's been sighted at Kettle Cove and I'm planning a trip there soon."

I could barely contain my excitement. "But after Uncle Lawrence gets done with me, I probably won't be allowed to go out anywhere," I wailed.

It was then that we struck our bargain. "I have some influence with Lawrence," he said. "I have known him since he was a boy."

What could I do? Benjamin Cleveland and I had a bet about who would see the sea serpent first. Whoever lost must bring the other a present next time we met. So I promised. But I kept my fingers crossed behind my back as I did so.

Chapter Five

Uncle Lawrence set down the wooden bucket and rake and stood surveying the yard at Twenty-one Union Street. "It's a sin to waste food," he said.

"Yes, sir." With the exception of "come along with me," those were the first words he'd uttered to me all morning. He was absolutely daft over not wasting food. Aunt Mattie said he spent hours poring over records of emergency food rations for every town militia in Massachusetts.

"Take the bucket and start picking up."

I couldn't believe he expected *me* to do such work. But, I should have known, as head of the state militia, he wasn't about to coddle me.

"Start with the eggshells. Put them in the bucket."

I did so. Out of the corner of my eye I saw him take off his coat, loosen his silk cravat, roll up his sleeves, and start to pick up the broken crock pieces. Aunt Mattie once said he never asked his men to do anything he wouldn't do himself. I supposed I should be honored to be treated as one of his men.

We worked in silence. He seemed angry. At me? Or at Aunt Hannah for pulling him away from his work? I knew he was a very important man. He took orders only from the governor. And Aunt Hannah.

Soon everything in the front yard was cleaned up. He took the chicken from the tree. Then he handed me a rag to wipe my hands. "Now we must clean off the front of the house. Go knock at the door and ask for a bucket of water."

"The well is right over there."

"I know that. But we don't use it until we ask permission."

He was a very tall man. Though he was forty-two, he had the energy of someone years younger. He was my father's older brother. *He must have gotten all the confidence in the family*, I thought. *There was none left for my father.*

I knocked on the door. Scuffling sounds came from inside.

"Look lively! Spaniards on deck! Spaniards on deck!" That was Georgie's parrot, Octavius.

She kept creatures. She took in wounded animals. Rabbits and squirrels were her regulars, though she wasn't above a raccoon or two. Her house was full of birds in cages, some very exotic.

The door opened. She was holding The Prophet, her huge, one-eyed, gray-and-black-striped cat. With the other hand she held a corn-cob pipe.

The Prophet growled. She'd named him after Tecumseh's brother.

"Good morning, Georgie. I've brought you more food." I set the bundle down.

"You're not leaving it for the wolves this time?"

"There are no wolves hereabouts."

"There are humans worse than wolves. In the Northwest, where I come from, the wolf is our brother. Here nobody is."

I sighed. "You come from Grandfather's house. As I do." She was attempting to talk like an Indian again. In that stilted way I supposed Indians had when they spoke English. And except for having an Indian mother who'd been killed when she was a baby, she'd been raised as white as I.

She peered over my shoulder. "Is that Lawrence?"

"Uncle Lawrence," I corrected.

"He looks addled."

"He's a very busy man and he's come to clean up the mess."

"I know how busy he is. Training his militia to fight my people."

"Your people are at our house on Derby Street." I could smell liquor on her breath. She was dressed in some old Indian garb. Her long hair was dirty and swung loose. She looked nothing like the adored older cousin I used to know.

"My people are on the frontier," she said. "And

William Henry Harrison wants to kill them. Is *he* working for Harrison?" She pointed to Uncle Lawrence.

"The Shawnee are not your people, Georgie," I said patiently. "There is no profit in pretending."

"Who are my people then?"

"We are. Aunt Hannah and the family."

She gave a short, bitter laugh. "Your people, maybe, but not mine. You come around here, all prim and proper in your fine dress, dropping off poor bundles. Why doesn't anybody else from the family come?"

I had no answer for that. I just stared at her.

"Wait until you find out what kind of people they are, your wonderful family."

Again, I stood mute. I'm not good at conjuring up answers. I have to go home first and think about things for about three days.

"When Tecumseh unites all the tribes, I will go back. They will be one nation then. Stronger than the United States are. They will want me in this nation. You will see."

Then she closed the door in my face.

I knocked again. "Georgie, I need to use the well."

No answer. I knocked harder. "Georgie!"

The door opened. And before I knew what was happening a stream of cold water hit me in the face. I gasped, reached and flailed, and fell back in a clatter on the rickety wooden steps.

"Oh, you'll pay for that, Georgie! You will!"

Laughter from within. "You know where the well is."

In the next moment Uncle Lawrence was beside me. I scrambled to my feet. My hair and face and the front of my dress were dripping. I was crying. He helped me up and wiped me off.

"Did you see what she *did*?" I sputtered. "She's a mindless idiot. You saw it. Now you know."

"I had no idea that she and this place were in such a sorry state. I've been too busy with my militia to pay mind."

"Is that all you care about? She wants it that way. She's crazier than a hooty owl! And she drinks and smokes opium in that pipe of hers. And *sailors* visit her from the wharves."

My rage made me weak. "And Aunt Hannah went and named her after George Washington! They should let her go to the Indians. Why don't they let her?"

"Hush. I'm sorry. No more now, Elizabeth." He scowled and shook his head. "Come along."

I followed him into the backyard where he found a shovel, dug a hole, and buried the remains of the food. Then he filled the bucket at the well. He found some strong soap. He worked on the front of the house. I stood watching him for a while. He didn't give me any more orders. After about ten minutes, I started in helping him.

We both worked with a vengeance. Through a hole in the fence I saw little Nathaniel Hathorne watching us. But I said nothing. And if Uncle Lawrence saw him, he said nothing, either.

On the way home he started talking. "We must do something about that place. It's a disgrace to our family."

"Georgie says she's going back west. When Tecumseh unites all the tribes. And they'll be stronger than the United States are."

He stopped walking. "We're not an *are*, Elizabeth," he said, "we're an *is*."

I looked at him.

"We must think of the United States as an *is*. As one people. That is what Tecumseh is trying to do with the Indians. Georgie is right. And if he succeeds, we're in trouble."

I didn't care about Tecumseh. I was sick to the teeth of hearing about him. "Do you think it's right for Uncle Louis to bring home this half-Indian girl? Considering what happened to Georgie?"

"This one claims to be Thankful's daughter. If she is, we must welcome her and make a place for her."

"What do you suppose Grandfather will think of her?"

"If she can prove she is Thankful's daughter, I'm sure he'll be beside himself with joy."

"But she's half-Indian."

He looked pained. And I recollected what Aunt

Hannah had said once, that Uncle Lawrence blamed himself for Aunt Thankful's capture. She said no more. That's the trouble with my family. They say things like that and don't elaborate. And I'm left with wild imaginings about them all.

"Yes," he said, "well, it won't be easy for any of us, Elizabeth. We have set feelings against the Indians. And what happened to Thankful doesn't help any. But we are going to have to re-examine our thinking. And give this girl a chance."

"What if she can't prove she's Aunt Thankful's daughter?"

"Well, in heaven's name, Ebie, why would she come to Salem, of all places, and to your godforsaken house in particular, if she weren't?"

I had no answer for that.

"She won't get very far with your grandfather, if she can't prove who she is. And if that happens, she won't suffer to stay."

Exactly, I thought.

"I hope you intend to keep an open mind concerning her, Elizabeth."

"Oh, yessir," I lied.

"You must try. Because we all owe it to Thankful."

I said yessir again. But the debt was not mine. I owed nothing. If anything, I thought they all owed something to me for what they had allowed to happen to them because of Thankful.

But I said nothing. Uncle Lawrence had his demons. Ever since I'd found the Indian paintings,

I knew that. And he also had a streak of honor pulling at him. Aunt Mattie said it was as strong as the moon pulling at the tide. Being Uncle Richard's little sister, she knows a lot about things like honor and tides. She also said that men like Uncle Lawrence, plagued with scruples and integrity, can be a burden to those around them. And then she heaved a great sigh. I now knew why.

Chapter Six

When we got home, everyone was in the back parlor. And there was a lively discussion going on. I went upstairs to change and when I came back down I stood in the hallway, listening.

John Gardener was in there, too. He'd been with Aunt Hannah forever, her groom and all-around man. Now he was setting up a quilt frame.

"Please, Mattie," Aunt Hannah was saying, "I know what the quilt looks like. I worked on it most of my young years."

"All the more reason you should think about finishing it," Aunt Mattie argued.

"I don't see why. Whatever possessed you to bring it down from the attic after so many years?"

"The girl Louis is bringing," Aunt Mattie said. "Don't you remember how Thankful took her part of the quilt west?"

"I want to forget anything to do with those years," Aunt Hannah said.

"Nonsense," from Uncle Lawrence. "They were good years, Hannah."

"They were not good, Lawrence. Not in this house."

"Well, you made them so for us," he told her.

That mollified Aunt Hannah somewhat. I heard her sigh. She is a person who likes sympathy. And she will say certain things just to hear Uncle Lawrence and Aunt Mattie tell her she is mistaken, that she is so much better than all that.

Listening to my elders is better than going to see the wax displays of the human body in the Sun Tavern, where they show you the heart and the brain. I learn all about human hearts and brains right here at home.

"I can't help thinking it was this quilt that gave Father the notion to start his mill. And every day, when I see those little children pricking their fingers in the machinery, I feel guilty," Aunt Hannah said.

"You're doing much good for those children," Lawrence reminded her.

"Just seeing the quilt again reminds me of Abby and Thankful. No, I want no part of it. Put the frame back upstairs, John, please."

John Gardener came out of the room carrying the cumbersome frame. He winked as he walked by me. Aunt Mattie said something then, but I didn't catch it. Cecie dropped a pan in the kitchen. The trouble with eavesdropping is that all kinds of noises interfere and when you pick up the drift of the conversation it's like having to start all over with your knitting after you've dropped six stitches.

"You don't want Louis to see her like that, do you?" Uncle Lawrence asked.

"No," Aunt Hannah replied. "I know the place must be cleaned up. I was thinking of asking John and Cecie. John's brother can help, too. And I think Ebie should. It will do her good."

"Do you think that's wise?" Uncle Lawrence asked, "the way Georgie treats her?"

The town crier went by, then, ringing his bell and saying something about a ship being sighted off Naugus Head.

". . . you know I never make any decision regarding Ebie without first asking you," Aunt Hannah was saying. "But I think some retribution on her part is in order."

"Well, all right then," from Uncle Lawrence. "Ebie? I know you're out there listening. Come on in."

I went in. Aunt Hannah left the room to oversee supper. Aunt Mattie stood up. She was holding the quilt, running her hands over it.

All my life I'd heard about this quilt that Aunt Hannah and her sisters were working on when they were parted. Aunt Abigail had taken her piece of it to sea and had been shipwrecked with it. Still had it, too. Aunt Abigail hadn't been home since she eloped. Aunt Hannah had visited her once, on her plantation on St. Helena's Island, off the coast of South Carolina. She'd taken me with her, but I can scarce remember it.

I'd played with a boy cousin. I supposed that was Jemmy, the one who was always supposed to come and see us but never did.

The quilt didn't look like much of anything to me. Just some patchwork of fabric of every color and description.

"I suppose I must take this back upstairs," Aunt Mattie said wistfully.

"For now, Mattie, yes," Uncle Lawrence said.

Aunt Mattie's face was set in a pout as she left the room. I stood in front of Uncle Lawrence.

"You are to go with Cecie and John Gardener, on a day to be decided upon, and help clean up Georgie's house," he said.

"Why?"

He seemed at a loss for words. I supposed that no one ever asked him why when he told them to do something. "It will make you appreciate what you have," he said.

"I mean why does the place have to be cleaned for Uncle Louis? Why keep from him the way things are?"

He scowled. "Don't make things difficult. As long as Aunt Hannah wants to keep trying with Georgie, we must help her."

"You mean as long as she wants to keep lying to Uncle Louis."

"I will not take sass, Ebie." His voice was even

and low. "You are too young to understand. Now do I have your promise that you will cooperate?"

For only a second, I wondered what he would do if I said no. I'd wondered before with Uncle Lawrence. Then he'd look at me, into my eyes. And I'd become sensible of the fact that there was no saying no to this man. He was confident in his rightness. Beyond him there was only God to answer to. And if you answered to him, God wouldn't call you to account.

"Yessir."

"Good."

"May I ask Mary to help?"

"I'd rather we kept this in the family, Ebie."

"Mary is a good influence on me, Uncle Lawrence. Even Aunt Hannah says so."

His mouth twitched, like it was a struggle for him to stay looking stern. But he'd had a lot of practice at it. "Very well. Just be patient with Aunt Hannah. She's anxious over Louis coming for a visit. And meeting this girl. I know I can count on you, Ebie, don't prove me wrong."

At supper Aunt Hannah was still vexed with me. "Eat your soup, Ebie," she said sharply.

"I don't like turtle soup."

"The mill children would give a week's wages for a bowl of it."

The mill children were her favorite weapon over me. She was always telling me how lucky I was because I didn't have to suffer their lot.

"They won't have a week's wages to give soon," Uncle Lawrence said. "I had a letter from Father today. He and his friend, Francis Cabot Lowell, have been visiting British factories and stealing secrets. Like Slater did twenty years ago."

"Must we talk about the mills at supper?" Aunt Mattie asked.

"He's seen advances in machine weaving," Uncle Lawrence went on. "He proposes to put all the spinning and weaving machines under one roof, have southern cotton delivered at one end of the factory, and bales of finished yard goods come out the other."

"What has all this dreary business to do with the mill children?" Aunt Hannah asked.

"There will be no more children," Uncle Lawrence said. "For this task he will need young women."

"He had young girls when he started more than twenty years ago. There was nothing but trouble. Ebie, finish your soup," Aunt Hannah said again.

But I was slumped down in my chair, already turned in on myself. Talk of the mills made me melancholy. Because it brought up my mother's family. They knew it, all of them, but they kept taking the past out like a piece of old bread dough, kneading it until it took the shape they wanted.

Sooner or later, my grandfather Brown's name would come into all this mill talk. Because their discussions always went way back. I knew the story by heart.

About the time, twenty years ago, when Grandfather Chelmsford's first little cotton yarn manufactory was failing because Americans preferred the cheaper British cotton, a sly fox of a man named Samuel Slater brought British cotton-making secrets to America. Inside his head.

In Rhode Island he met Moses Brown, my other grandfather, who was an even slyer fox. Together they set up a mill to make cotton yarn. But Americans still wanted the cheaper British item.

So Brown got in touch with my grandfather Chelmsford, who always knew a better way to skin a cat, and they wrote a petition to Congress and got duties on imported cotton raised.

In order to do this, Brown came to Salem. With him he brought his beautiful daughter, Emily.

My mother.

Of course, Grandfather Chelmsford got something out of it. He talked Brown into letting him in on those British cotton-making secrets, too. Within a year, Grandfather Brown and Grandfather Chelmsford were both doing so well that they had to get agents to sell the cloth made by hand weavers from their yarns.

Within three years my father had married Emily Brown. He was only eighteen at the time.

Somehow, their meeting and marrying and having me is all mixed up inside me with the success of both mills. And the little children who get their hands stuck in the machinery every day.

"Sit up straight, Ebie," Aunt Hannah said.

"Take away her soup, Cecie," Uncle Lawrence directed.

Cecie did so. Uncle Lawrence heaped my plate with meat and potatoes. I ate. They took up their conversation.

"Where will Father get the money?" Aunt Hannah asked.

"Lowell's brother-in-law is getting it," Uncle Lawrence said. "They will incorporate the Boston Manufacturing Company."

"I should have let the do-good women of Salem close that manufactory down years ago," Aunt Hannah said.

Once, she had saved Grandfather Chelmsford's original manufactory from being closed down. I never understood how. I did understand that she regretted it.

"When will Father be home, then, Lawrence?" she asked.

"Within six weeks."

"What will happen to the mill children now?" Only Aunt Mattie would think to ask such a question.

Uncle Lawrence suggested asking Parson Bentley to help resettle them. They started talking about that then.

I could think of only one thing. I had six weeks to get rid of the Indian girl before Grandfather came home. And she wasn't even here yet.

Chapter Seven

Late October 1811

The town fathers were pushing to have Georgie put away. I didn't know it. I didn't even know what being put away meant. Mary had to explain it to me.

"In Salem's almshouse," she said, "where they keep some who are mad. Or in the private home in Chatham, run by Abraham Goodele."

Her blue eyes were solemn with the knowledge and the sadness of it, as she said the words to me. "My brother Moses met your uncle Lawrence at the Blue Heron Tavern yesterday afternoon and told him," she said.

Isn't that the way of it, though? Probably everybody in my family knew it but me. Though I'd been sent to help John Gardener and Cecie clean up Twenty-one Union Street that day.

Mary and I were standing in the dingy kitchen when she told me that. We were trying to get Georgie and all her animals outside.

"Spaniards on deck!" Octavius was screeching from his cage. "Spaniards on deck! Look lively!"

I supposed we looked like Spaniards to him. We were intruders.

"I'll take him," Georgie said. And she reached up, opened the cage, and took him out. He nestled on her shoulder. "We're going to the quarterdeck, you old dear," she said. "Don't you worry. I won't let the Spaniards hurt you."

Then she turned to me and Mary. "They can clean all they want to," she said of Cecie and John Gardener, who were waiting for us to take the animals outside, "but they can't take my birds. They can't take my cats. Or my raccoons. I don't care about my father coming. I don't want to see him."

"Raccoons?" Mary whispered to me. "She has *raccoons?*"

Somehow, we got the animals and birds out in the backyard. Georgie huddled with them. Occasionally, she would get up and curse at John Gardener and Cecie in Spanish. Then in French.

Mary and I had the job of settling her down, keeping her out of the house, and fetching buckets of water to bring inside.

Fetching the water was the easy part. But finally we got Georgie quiet.

At the well, I looked at Mary. "Georgie isn't crazy," I said. "She's just Georgie."

"Just the same, Moses says there are laws on the books. And people know how to use them to have others put away when they want. Remember James Snow?"

"The man who chased us through his yard with a piece of broken glass?"

Mary nodded. "He just happened to be fixing a broken window at the time. But all the children teased him to the point of distraction. Moses said Snow's neighbors signed a petition. He was deemed furiously mad and put in the almshouse for eight months."

We were silent for a moment.

"It would kill Aunt Hannah," I said.

"I don't think she knows about it, Ebie. I'm sure your uncle Lawrence hasn't told her."

I didn't know whether to be glad or sorry for Georgie, then. We carried the bucket of water together, back to the house. As we passed Georgie with Octavius on her shoulder, I whispered to Mary, "She *looks* mad. Anybody would take her for being crazier than a hooty owl."

"But we know she isn't," Mary said.

"It's because I'm sensible of what made her this way," I allowed.

"That makes all the difference," Mary agreed. "Knowing what goes into making a person the way he is. When you know that, you can forgive anything."

Almost anything, I thought. And then I wondered, *If I knew what went into making the Indian girl what she was, would I forgive her for wanting to come into our family?*

I decided I wouldn't. I was not as good a person as Mary. I think I knew that all along.

"Your uncle told Moses it won't take much more for the town fathers to put Georgie away," Mary said. "So don't trifle with her anymore, Ebie. You don't want to be responsible for it happening, do you?"

I decided that not even I was that bad. And I said no, I didn't.

But I was still furious at Uncle Lawrence for not telling me about it.

I didn't see him for three days. But I was determined to let him know about it.

We were in the parlor. Uncle Louis was due any minute with the Indian girl and we were all half-daft, waiting.

"I'm serving everything they had at the banquet Louis attended in Philadelphia back in '96," Aunt Hannah said. "When President Washington feted the Indian chiefs."

And for about the tenth time she went over the menu. "Roasted turkey, suckling pig, a large baked fish, vegetables, fruit, cake, Madeira, nuts, cider, Marlborough pie."

I'd made the Marlborough pie. It was my specialty.

"All that will be missing are the Indian chiefs," Uncle Lawrence said.

"Don't brood, Lawrence," Aunt Hannah said. Then to Aunt Mattie, "Do I look all right?"

"Beautiful." Aunt Mattie looked up from her knitting. She sighed, and I knew what she was thinking. Too beautiful. Poor Richard.

Aunt Hannah was wearing a new rose-colored silk gown that I'd never seen before. I supposed this was her greeting-an-old-flame-from-the-west gown.

"What will Louis think of me? I've aged."

"So has he," Uncle Lawrence reminded her.

"Oh, dear." Aunt Hannah got up and for about the tenth time looked at her image in the gilt-edged mirror. "Georgie should be here to greet her father. Did you remember to invite her, Ebie?"

"Yes, ma'am."

"What did she say?"

"That she would rather walk over hot coals than see him."

"I must attend to the punch bowl." And she hurried from the room.

I turned to Uncle Lawrence. "Doesn't it seem that Aunt Hannah speaks more of Uncle Louis than Uncle Richard?"

"Well, your uncle Richard never met two presidents. Nor has he been adopted by the Miami tribe."

"But he's asked her to marry him five times. And Uncle Louis asked only once."

"The preoccupation you have with Richard marrying your aunt is not new, Ebie," he said. "Your father took it upon himself to do the same thing when he was young, too."

"He did?" I asked.

"Yes. And to what end? I'm convinced your

aunt Hannah will never marry. She likes being a spinster."

"Well, you're in a fine fettle," Aunt Mattie said.

"I'm not in any kind of a fettle. I just know my sister."

But we were all in a fettle, nervous as hungry cats at a clambake.

"She'll marry, and she'll marry Richard. No woman likes being a spinster," Aunt Mattie insisted.

"I'm just afraid Uncle Louis will walk in here all browned like a frontiersman and Aunt Hannah will lose her senses," I said.

Those were Mary's words, not mine.

"He's a hero," I went on. "He prevented an Indian massacre at Fort Wayne last spring. Aunt Hannah will lose her senses as soon as he walks in the door. And Uncle Richard is wasting away on a British prison ship. It isn't fair."

"Then I'll make sure she regains those senses," Aunt Mattie said.

"It isn't for you two to concern yourselves with," Uncle Lawrence said, "you're just a child, Ebie."

Well, that was what I'd been waiting for. I jumped on him like a cat on a wharf rat. "I'm *not* a child. I know more than I let on. I know the town fathers want to put Georgie away."

"Away?" Aunt Mattie stopped knitting. "Lawrence, you didn't tell me." Her voice was full of reproach.

Good. He was in trouble with Aunt Mattie now. It served him right.

"It's only talk," he said.

"Larry. Dear God, you must not let this happen."

"Mattie?" Aunt Hannah called from the dining room. "Come help me with these seating arrangements."

Aunt Mattie got up and put her knitting aside. "Lawrence," she said.

He looked up at her. Something passed between them. And I saw that he answered to her, too. But that he didn't answer to her authority, like the governor's, or her shrillness, like Aunt Hannah's, but to her gentleness. It puzzled me.

He placated her and she left the room. "Now see what you've done," he scolded. "Can't you leave well enough be, Ebie. Don't we have enough to worry us around here?"

"You should have told me, Uncle Lawrence. I had to find out from Mary. You sent me over there to clean up. I had a right to know."

He looked at me. "If there was anything to tell you, I'd tell you," he said. "And as far as being grown-up, well, a grown-up knows what not to say in front of some people."

He was angry. I knew better than to provoke him any further. *I know what not to say in front of some people*, I thought. *Did I tell you that Aunt Hannah and Uncle Louis were once lovers?*

Once, just once, she'd written in her journal, *we*

gave in to our passions. Ever after, our friendship has been chaste. And oh, I carry the torment of my guilt. God's invincible fury scourges me. I have sinned against Richard as if we were truly wed. How can I wed him now? I have vowed I will not be like my mother, I will not.

I did not understand what she meant about her mother. But I understood the rest. And I longed to tell Uncle Lawrence, to show him I knew when to keep quiet.

But I'd long since found out that too often we can't say the very thing that will redeem us. And if that isn't being grown-up, I don't know what is.

I'd promised Mary I would take note of everything Aunt Hannah did when she first saw Uncle Louis. Mary was keeping a journal. She scribbled in it everything of note that went on in Salem.

When the carriage pulled up in front, Uncle Louis got out first. He was dressed in fringed buckskins and boots. He had a pistol in his belt. As John Gardener untethered Uncle Louis's own horse from behind the carriage, Uncle Louis removed the saddlebags from its back and threw them over a broad shoulder.

He was very tall. His hair was long and dark and straight, tied behind and very clean. The fringe on his buckskin shirt danced as he moved. And those movements were spare and sure. I searched my head for another word. *Graceful?* Can a man be graceful?

Yes, I decided. And yes, Aunt Hannah will be swooning as soon as he walks in the door.

He turned to help the girl out of the carriage. He put a hand under her elbow as she stared up at the house.

She was very slender. She wore her dark hair in long braids and was dressed in a simple one-piece garment the color of butter. It looked like doeskin and had long fringe on the sleeves and at the hem of the skirt. She wore soft boots and a band studded with silver around her forehead.

I supposed she was beautiful. In a forest creature sort of way. She looked out of place on our street, like a gold leaf just dropped from a tree in a summer garden.

Uncle Louis leaned down and murmured something to her and they moved toward the steps.

"Merciful Father," Uncle Lawrence whispered.

I was standing next to him at the window and I looked up. His gaze was fixed on the girl as on an apparition. His face had gone slack. Tears brewed in his eyes.

The front door was flung open.

"Louis, my dear Louis!" Aunt Hannah ran into his arms.

"Hannah!" He dropped his saddlebags with a clatter. And he wrapped his arms around her.

I think I was the only one of all of them, including Cecie and John Gardener, who was not crying.

Chapter Eight

The girl was beautiful. There was no denying it. When she stepped into the light of the hall, I could see that. And I hated her on sight.

There was something so self-possessed about her. She moved in her own world, her own place. And it was a serene place. I could hate her for that alone.

She did not have one blue eye and one green one, though. I don't know if anyone else noticed that. I don't think any of them were looking to determine it.

"Welcome, Walking Breeze," Aunt Hannah said.

Introductions were made, clumsily. Nobody knew what to do next. Walking Breeze did. She reached amongst her things on the floor and drew out a gift. "For you." She handed it to Aunt Hannah.

"How lovely." But Aunt Hannah did not know what it was. Nobody did.

"It's a wampum belt," Uncle Louis explained.

"Indians always give them at important meetings. The different colored beads mean different things. The white beads are a symbol of peace. The yellow bird in the middle means good news. The covered bones mean forgiveness for those killed. Walking Breeze wove it for you."

Just what Aunt Hannah needed, I told myself, a wampum belt. Wait until I tell Mary.

Uncle Louis had gifts for everyone. Silver bracelets for me and Aunt Mattie, a gallon-sized pouch for Uncle Lawrence. Walking Breeze crossed the parlor to the chair where Uncle Lawrence sat and gave him the gift. Her bearing was very straight. You could tell that to her this was ceremony.

"Thank you," Uncle Lawrence said. But he barely looked at her. "What's inside the pouch?"

"Finely ground cornmeal mixed with syrup," Uncle Louis said. "We use it all the time. Add water for a rich gruel. You might think of having some made up for your militia's emergency rations."

Then Walking Breeze gave Aunt Hannah another gift, this one a large object wrapped in burlap.

Aunt Hannah's hands shook as she untied the rawhide and the burlap fell away. Then everyone gasped. Everyone except Uncle Lawrence. He just stared. On his face was the most devastated look I had ever seen.

It was a portrait of Uncle Louis, standing beside an Indian chief.

"That's Little Turtle, chief of the Miami tribe," Uncle Louis said. "He's the one who adopted me. The painting was done by Gilbert Stuart."

"It's beautiful," Uncle Lawrence said warmly. Then he fell silent. Everyone did.

"Coming from you, Lawrence, that's a compliment," Uncle Louis said. And that was worse than anything. Because it alluded to Uncle Lawrence's paintings.

The mood was as thick as the fog that ships floundered in off Naugus Head. And it set the tone for supper. Which was a disaster.

Uncle Lawrence continued to brood and to sneak glances at Walking Breeze when she wasn't looking. Aunt Mattie kept a running conversation going, afraid that if she stopped the silences would be so deep we would all fall into them.

Aunt Hannah couldn't keep her eyes off Uncle Louis. And he answered her questions in between helping Walking Breeze.

She needed to be helped. She didn't know how to act when Cecie came round with the different platters of food.

"Turkey," Uncle Louis would explain to her.

She shook her head no, vigorously.

"Pork," he said as he delicately laid a bit of suckling pig on her plate.

Again she shook her head no. She accepted some baked fish and vegetable. Everyone tried not to notice.

"So then, Louis, you are going to be reinstated as Indian agent at Fort Wayne," Aunt Hannah said.

"Yes." He smiled, explaining to us. "I was dismissed from the job two years ago because William Henry Harrison complained that I favored the Indians over the whites."

"Did you?" Uncle Lawrence asked.

Uncle Louis shrugged. "After all, I once had an Indian wife."

I thought it boorish of him to remind us of such.

"But he fought the Indians when the occasion warranted it," Aunt Hannah put in quickly. "And he redeemed himself in Harrison's eyes by preventing the Indian massacre at Fort Wayne in March. Which is why he was reinstated."

Uncle Lawrence was eyeing him narrowly. "It sounds like a confusing job. Like you don't know whether to stand for or against the Indians."

"Being an Indian agent has always required that one be able to see both sides," Uncle Louis said. "I argued with Harrison over the way he was cheating the Miamis out of their land. And then I convinced Little Turtle not to let his people support Tecumseh's confederation."

Walking Breeze was struggling with her fork. Use of it was new to her, I could see. "Remember what I taught you," I heard Uncle Louis whisper. Then she dropped her fork on her plate at the mention of Tecumseh. She was getting agitated.

"How near are we to war on the frontier?" Uncle Lawrence asked.

"Perhaps we should let Walking Breeze answer that," Uncle Louis said.

Everyone looked at her. Slowly she raised her eyes from her plate. "The face of war has been seen all over the land for the last five years," she said quietly.

It seemed as if the candles on the tables flickered. It was eerie, the way she said it. I shivered.

Uncle Louis smiled. "Harrison is gobbling up millions of acres of Indian land and pushing the Indians into the camp of the British. He's a benighted fool. The Indians are being lied to and cheated. Old hurts from the last war by the British against the Americans are being uncovered. All last summer we had killings and unrest between whites and Indians in the Indiana territory. And in outlying districts of the Illinois territory."

"Are we to blame?" Uncle Lawrence asked.

"Both whites and Indians are to blame. But captured Indians bear new weapons given to them by the British."

I watched Walking Breeze. Again, I saw a quiet strength about her. I envied it.

"And the Indians tell us there will soon be a great uprising," Uncle Louis went on. "Tecumseh has managed to unite almost all the tribes. He can muster fifty or a hundred thousand Indians to rise at once against us. The Indians are awaiting his sign."

"What sign?" Aunt Mattie asked. Her blue eyes were round and frightened.

"We don't know," Uncle Louis said. "Tecumseh told Harrison in their last meeting in July that he would return from his trip south in spring. But we think he will return before then. In December. That's when the sign is to be given."

Was I the only one to see the secret smile creep across Walking Breeze's lips?

"Do you believe in the sign?" Uncle Lawrence asked.

"I think we should stop all this war talk," Aunt Mattie said. "It's upsetting Walking Breeze."

"She's been raised on war talk," Uncle Louis said. "It doesn't matter, to answer the question, if no whites believe in this sign, Lawrence. The Indians do. Tecumseh once prophesied an eclipse and it came. They believe in his powers. And in those of his brother, The Prophet."

"Why do they call him The Prophet?" Aunt Hannah asked.

"Because he claims to have visions and special medicine."

"The Prophet is a fool!" Walking Breeze blurted out.

Everyone stared at her. Cecie, who had been clearing away the dishes, near dropped a platter of fish.

"You know this Prophet?" Aunt Hannah asked.

She nodded. "I and my mother were living under the protection of Tecumseh," she said in a

— 74 —

clear, firm voice. "Tecumseh bade his brother to keep the peace in his absence. The Prophet did not heed him. He allowed warriors to steal some white men's horses."

Everyone was staring at her. She saw their stares and faltered.

"Go on, Walking Breeze," Uncle Louis urged.

"Forgive me if my face is full of storm," she said. "When trouble came because of the horse stealing, The Prophet gave me to the whites. I did not wish to be given over. I did it for Tecumseh, who is big in my heart. So the peace he worked for wouldn't be broken."

"Dear child," Aunt Mattie said.

"Did Tecumseh treat you and your mother well?" Aunt Hannah asked. I could see tears in her eyes as she said it.

"My mother died happy," Walking Breeze said simply. Clearly, she would say no more of the matter. She lowered her eyes, and it was as if she had closed a door on that subject.

Silence fell over the table. Uncle Lawrence accepted a cup of coffee from Aunt Hannah, who was pouring from the silver pot Cecie had brought in on a tray.

"How can Tecumseh align himself with the British after the way they treated the Indians at the Battle of Fallen Timbers back in '94?" he asked. "I was there with General Wayne. The British closed the gates of Fort Miami against the Indians and left them deserted when Wayne attacked."

"Tecumseh offered to fight with us against the British if his land was returned," Uncle Louis said. "But have you ever known us to give back land, Lawrence?"

"Mr. Louis," Walking Breeze said, "I have much *dah-quel-e-mah* for you. Because you brought me to my Shemanese family. But I would speak now. Or the words will rot in my heart."

"Speak, do," Uncle Louis said.

She looked around the table, from one of us to the other. "Tecumseh does not wish to fight on the side of any white man, British or Shemanese," she said. "All he wants is to be given back his land on the Wabash that the white chief Harrison bought from some Miamis who were drunk with Shemanese stupid water and who had no right to sell it. That land is our best hunting ground."

No one spoke. Or even moved. Aunt Hannah ran her tongue over her lips, which were dry. Uncle Lawrence stared outright at Walking Breeze, seeing what? Aunt Mattie's eyes bulged.

"And now that I have spoken, I am tired. I would find my pallet."

"Of course, child," Aunt Hannah said. "How thoughtless of us. I'm putting you in my sister Abby's room. Cecie will direct John Gardener to carry your things upstairs and fetch hot water." She was rambling. She knew how flighty she sounded in the presence of this young girl who spoke so simply of things like truth rotting in the heart.

"Ebie," she said, "take our guest to her room."

I got up from the table. Walking Breeze followed. Uncle Lawrence and Uncle Louis stood up as she left the room.

Uncle Lawrence never did that for me, I minded.

Walking Breeze started up the stairs. "I'll be along in a minute," I said. And I ran back into the dining room to fetch my unfinished cake.

"What is *dah-quel-e-mah?*" Aunt Mattie was asking.

"Love," Uncle Louis said. "Family love."

"What's Shemanese?" said Aunt Hannah.

"American."

"What is your standing with Tecumseh?" Uncle Lawrence inquired. "Can't you do something to prevent this uprising?"

"Tecumseh now despises me and considers me a traitor, because I convinced the Miamis not to support him," Uncle Louis answered. "I admire the man. But I have recommended to Harrison that he be assassinated. Before it is too late."

Chapter Nine

Something was not right. As we mounted the stairs, my thoughts played tricks on me, like the shadows and light cast from the candles in the wall sconces.

Uncle Louis was deceptive. He accepted this girl's *dah-quel-e-mah*, yet he'd admitted that he had recommended to Harrison that Tecumseh be assassinated. When he knew how much Walking Breeze loved the man.

I don't know what led me to ask the question. Mary would say I had uncommon powers. "How long have you known my uncle Louis?"

"Two moons. Since I sought him out at Fort Wayne."

"How did you know to seek him out?"

"My mother told me to when she was dying. She and Mr. Louis were friends from many years before. He had not been to our village since I was a small child. But always, his scouts brought greetings to my mother from him when they visited."

Then Uncle Louis had known all these years that

Aunt Thankful was alive. Why had he kept that truth from us?

That's what was wrong! No one had thought to ask Uncle Louis why the girl had sought him out. They all assumed she had just been brought in to Fort Wayne.

Least of all, Hannah. She trusted him. Because they had once been *lovers.* But he had kept from her, this truth.

Why?

I sensed it had to do with the fact that this girl was not Aunt Thankful's true daughter, but an imposter. And that Uncle Louis knew it.

Aunt Hannah had outdone herself with Aunt Abby's room. There was a new crewel bedcover with matching bed hangings, and a feather quilt. The floor had been polished to a rich luster and a Brussels carpet brought from below stairs. The gleaming copper tub that was mine sat before the hearth where Cecie had a brisk fire going.

Cecie was setting out scented soap. "Come right on in, dearie. John's brought up your bundles and gone for one last pail of hot water. I'll leave you now. I must attend to the rest of supper."

"Where is my pallet?" Walking Breeze asked when Cecie had left the room.

"Your pallet?"

"I cannot sleep in that." She gestured to the bed.

"But you must sleep there. Aunt Hannah went

through a great deal of trouble for you."

Walking Breeze went to the bed and commenced to remove the crewel cover and bed linens. Then she began to tug at the mattress. "Will you help me?"

She'd already tugged the mattress half off. "You can't do that!" I protested.

She gave one final tug and the mattress landed on the floor.

I stood openmouthed as she pushed the copper tub aside and moved the mattress near to the hearth. For a slender girl, she certainly had strength.

John Gardener came in with the last bucket of hot water. He surveyed the damage, but said nothing. He poured the water into the tub, winked at me, and left.

"You can't sleep on the floor," I told her.

"Why?"

But I could think of no good reason why. Except that Aunt Hannah wouldn't like it. I'd always longed to sleep on the floor in front of the hearth in my room. But I had never dared.

She proceeded to empty the contents of her bundles. Out came a red blanket, soft moccasins, a pair of silver ear bobs, a small sack of corn, an earthenware bowl, and a sheathed knife.

"Aunt Hannah won't like that knife, either."

Out of the second bundle came another dress, this of a rougher fabric than the one she wore, a sack containing beads, a large buffalo robe, a fragment of deer hide, and a piece of quilting.

A piece of quilting.

Hardly that. Some pieces in it resembled the quilting Aunt Mattie had recently brought down from the garret. But they were faded and worn. Other pieces had been added, bits of primitive matter that I could not name.

"This," she said and she held up the quilting, "was my mother's. From her time with the She-manese. From when she lived here. In Mass-a-chus-etts."

My head was spinning. Thoughts crackled inside it like the fire in the hearth, making it hurt. Yes, I had a throbbing headache. And my face felt feverish. Perhaps I was coming down with something.

Fear. I was coming down with a good dose of the blue devils, as Mary would call it. One thought alone becalmed me.

I would get rid of this piece of quilting. I could not let Aunt Hannah see it. It was an abomination. Nothing less. It embodied everything that had driven them to their obsessions and peculiarities. And bedeviled them.

And then another thought came to me. "Why didn't you give this to Aunt Hannah before? When you first came in our door?"

She shook her head. "The time must be right. I must first open a path from her to me. I must remove the logs, brush, and briars from that path."

She isn't sure about the quilting, I thought. *Because she isn't Thankful's daughter.*

I understood then. Likely, she lived in the same village. And knew my aunt Thankful. And took the quilting from her so she could pass herself off as belonging to my family. Because when The Prophet put her out, she had no place to go.

Well, I would end it all, before it started. Before we brought another Georgie down on all our heads.

"Let's put your things away," I suggested. I looked around. I must hide the quilt. Anywhere for now. I could retrieve it and get rid of it later. Then I saw the chest of drawers in the corner.

"Here, we'll put your things away in these drawers." In the bottom drawer I put the piece of quilt. And I covered it with the red blanket.

"No one will touch your things here. And you should keep them hidden. Because Aunt Hannah wants you to be Shemanese. You want to please her, don't you?"

She nodded vigorously.

Then another thought came to me. "Did you show the quilting to Uncle Louis?"

"No. It would be as smoke to him. But to Hannah, it will be like fire."

"Yes," I said. "Well, let's keep the fire banked for a while. Until you clear the logs, brush, and briars from the path."

She agreed. And we packed everything away.

"Now you must bathe before the water cools. And put on this nightdress and get to your pallet." I scrambled to my feet, took a long flannel, lace-trimmed nightdress from a chair, and held it up for her.

She snorted with contempt. "I bathe only in Methtoqui. The creek or river. You have water here. I smelled it outside your house."

"That's the harbor. Where the ships come in."

"Ah," she said and she smiled. "The great canoes with wings."

In spite of myself I smiled, too. "Yes. But you can't bathe in the harbor. It's not seemly."

"Seem-ly?"

"There are strange men around. They will see you."

This she understood. Her face darkened with some fear. She stood up, and went to the copper tub, and tested the water with her fingers. Then she picked up the scented soap, sniffed it, and made a face.

I turned to get a large piece of flannel from a low stool. "Scented soap is a luxury," I told her. "You can dry yourself with this. I'll put another log on the fire and leave you to your privacy."

As I picked up the log, I heard a swift movement. The log settled, sending up sparks. I secured it with a smaller one, and turned.

She stood there naked before me. The doeskin dress lay in a crumpled heap on the floor.

I gasped. She stood, straight and proud. The

firelight played across her body. I could not help looking at her. She was very much a woman already. She held her chin high, smiling at me.

I went hot and cold. Never had I seen anyone naked. "You mustn't," I said.

She sensed my discomfort and laughed. "I will bathe for Hannah," she said. And she stepped into the tub.

Why, I thought, *she's worse than Georgie!* "I'll get you some warm milk and honey so you can sleep," I said. And I ran from the room, down the stairs. *Dear God,* I thought, *what creature is this who has come into our house?*

I felt the outrage of my Puritan ancestry. She went against the grain of everything we stood for. And I knew that I had to get her out. Soon.

Chapter Ten

"Do you love your father?" Uncle Louis asked me.

"I beg your pardon, sir?" It was too early. I did not understand the question at first. Outside dampness wrapped itself around the house. The hall clock struck six. Cecie fussed with the fire, coaxing some warmth into the dining room. Candles cast shadows. The clip-clopping of the fish vendor's horse and cart was the only sound in the street.

"I said, do you love your father?" He looked across the table at me.

Tears came to my eyes. "Yes."

"Good," he said, "good." Then he proceeded to eat the breakfast Cecie had set before him. Fresh eggs, broiled fish, cornbread, bean porridge, coffee.

"Eat," he said to me, "we've a big morning ahead of us."

I could not eat at this ungodly hour. The only reason I was up was because last night Aunt Hannah had said that someone must accompany Uncle Louis to Georgie's house this morning.

Of course that someone was me. When it came to Georgie, they always picked me to do the dirty work in this family.

"I've packed a bundle of warm clothing for her. It's in the hallway downstairs," Aunt Hannah had said. Then, as an afterthought, "It's going to be difficult for Louis, seeing his daughter again. Be kind to him."

I'd hated climbing out of bed so early, when the house was still dark. The only consolation was that this terrible mission had presented me with the opportunity to get rid of the quilt.

It was perfect, so perfect that I had the eerie feeling that fate had arranged it for me. Fate doesn't often cooperate. Not with me, at least. I jumped at the chance.

Last night, late, I had crept into Walking Breeze's room and, without benefit of even a candle, had groped my way to the chest of drawers and retrieved the piece of quilting.

She was a sound sleeper. She never even heard me.

The quilting now lay buried in the bundle of clothing for Georgie that sat in the hall.

"How *is* your father?" Uncle Louis asked between bites.

"Well, sir. He's seeing a man in Parliament. To get Uncle Richard out of prison."

"I always liked Cabot. He was such an adventurous little boy. I always thought he should have gone to the frontier. He gave your aunt Hannah no end of concern, growing up, you know."

"Yessir." I picked at my food and ate.

Uncle Louis carried the bundle of clothing for Georgie. He would not hear of my carrying it, though he also had a package of his own for her.

I could tell he was getting more anxious by the minute as we walked to her house.

The morning mist was lifting and the sky in the east was pink. Gulls cried in the distance and candles still glowed in house windows. Everything was covered with dew and looked untouched and fresh.

"No school today?" he asked.

'No, sir. On account of it's Training Day. Uncle Lawrence is going to review the Salem cadets. They have new uniforms."

"You've grown up nicely, Ebie."

"Thank you," I said.

"My daughter hasn't."

I did not know what to say to that, so I said nothing.

"I haven't seen my daughter in five years. Not since my last visit here. Is she very bad?"

"Beg pardon, sir?"

"Come now. They try to keep it from me, but I've heard what an embarrassment she is to the family. It isn't your aunt's fault. Everything Georgie is doing is to get back at me, because I sent her home from the west when she was fourteen."

"Yes, sir," I said. But I thought Georgie was going above and beyond what anybody needed to do to show she hated her father. If he had asked me, I would have told him Georgie was using him as an excuse to do anything she pleased and get away with it. But he did not ask me.

"Does she hate me very much?"

He was getting even more anxious. *Some Indian fighter,* I thought, *who once stuffed the bullet hole in his wrist with buzzard feathers, and kept on fighting. He needs more than buzzard feathers now, doesn't he?*

"You might as well tell me what to expect. A man goes into battle, he has a right to know the odds."

So I told him. And I made no attempt to prettify it. "She said she would rather walk over hot coals than see you. She said she would throw you off the property if you came."

Then he said something I'll never forget. "If only I could do something good for her, I would do it," he said. "I would do anything to make things right for her again. If I thought dying would do it, I would die."

There wasn't anything I could say to that, so I kept a still tongue in my head.

Georgie started throwing things the moment we got through the front gate. She had an assortment of things ready. Old apples, sticks, even small rocks.

Uncle Louis was not disturbed. He directed me to stay at the gate, put his bundles down, and walked up the path toward her.

Uncle Lawrence had told me that once, when Uncle Louis was captured by the Miami Indians, before they decided they liked him, he'd had to run a gauntlet. The Indians formed two lines and made a person run through. And beat him with sticks and clubs.

Watching him now, I thought that Indian gauntlet had likely been easier. He held his arms up to shield his face, but he kept walking to the porch. And talking to Georgie in low tones.

"Now, Georgie, you don't want to do that. Why don't you stop it?"

But apparently she did want to do it. Very much. She just kept reaching and throwing. Several times she hit Uncle Louis with apples or sticks, but he just kept right on going until he reached that porch.

All the while, from just inside the front door, Octavius was screaming about Spaniards being on deck.

When Uncle Louis got to the front porch, Georgie attacked him with her hands. She beat at his face and chest, flailing her arms wildly.

"Georgie, Georgie," he said with great sadness in his voice, "there is no profit in this. Why can't we just talk? I'm your father and I love you. Please, won't you listen to what I have to say?"

I had to look away then. Because I thought of

my own father. And how I would die first before I'd ever give him cause to speak to me like that.

Uncle Louis subdued her. He held her wrists firmly. She whimpered and broke away from him, ran into the house, and slammed the door.

"It's that cursed opium she smokes," he said as he came back down the walk. "I smelled it on her. Likely, she gets it from sailors who visit."

So he knew about the sailors then. I said nothing.

"The Indians smoke another form of it in a weed. It makes them crazy." He took the bundles to the steps, set them down, and stood there for a moment trying to decide what course of action to take. He called out to her again, rapped at the door, then on a window. There was no reply.

I went down the walk. All I wanted was that Georgie should take the bundle with the quilting in it.

"I can treat with the Indians," he was saying, "but I can't talk to my own daughter. It's what comes from lying, Ebie. I've been living a big lie all these years and nobody knows it."

Well, I could have told him that.

"Come on, let's go."

We went back out into the street. All the while my mind was on Aunt Hannah's bundle. *Suppose boys came again and tossed the contents in the yard?*

I needn't have worried. No sooner had we started to walk away than the door opened, and

Georgie whisked the bundles inside. She was nothing if not greedy.

"I stayed out on the frontier when Thankful was taken," Uncle Louis was saying. "I should have come home and seen to my daughter's care. Do you know why I stayed?"

I breathed a sigh of relief because the quilt was now in the house. I said no sir, I didn't.

"Because I found Thankful alive. She refused to come home. She wanted to stay and live with the Indians."

I stared at him in disbelief. "How could she *want* to stay with the Indians?"

"It happens sometimes with people who have been taken. I couldn't tell anyone. Especially not your grandfather. Because I knew he would never believe that his darling Thankful wouldn't come home to him. And for another reason."

I waited.

"Because he promised that my Georgie could have a home as long as I kept searching for Thankful. So I pretended to keep searching."

If it is possible to speak while you hold your breath, that is how I asked the next question. "Did you know that my aunt Thankful had a daughter?"

He shook his head and sighed. "I went back to her village once or twice and saw her after the child was born. So I knew she had a daughter, yes. But I stopped going when the child was about three. I couldn't go without begging Thankful to return home. I knew I was making things difficult for her and Cat-That-Prowls, her husband."

"So," I said carefully, "then you don't know if Walking Breeze *is* her daughter."

"I never claimed to know that, Ebie. She did call the child Walking Breeze."

But, I thought, *anyone can steal a name.*

He went on talking, saying something about how Aunt Thankful had made a life for herself with the Shawnees and he had no right to ruin it for her.

"Then I made a life for myself out there. I've a home and farm, livestock, slaves, and cornfields. I've got a good government salary. In the end it was easier than coming home."

"You've got slaves?" I asked.

"Yes. Why?"

"Nothing." Aunt Hannah hated slavery.

He started talking then, about how it was different out there, how slavery was all right. "But some things we can never make all right," he said. "I lied to your aunt and uncle about being able to find their sister. But to what end? Georgie had a home, yes. I wanted that. I wanted to make her a fine Salem lady, like your aunt Hannah. But you can't make someone what they don't want to be. Then, of course, I should never have brought her west to visit me. That is what brought the whole thing to a head. She's neither fish nor fowl now. She doesn't know what she is."

And how will it be any different with this girl

you have brought into our midst, I wanted to ask. But I didn't.

"So I've a mind to set things straight now with your aunt. No more lying. Do you think she could abide the truth, Ebie?"

I looked up into his face. He was a handsome man. I could see how Aunt Hannah might be taken with him. And now he would go back to Aunt Hannah, all forlorn and afflicted, because Georgie had treated him so badly. And if there was one thing Aunt Hannah could not ignore, it was a man who was forlorn and afflicted.

"Oh, I'm sure she could abide the truth, Uncle Louis," I said.

He beamed down at me. I smiled back.

Oh, Uncle Richard, I said to myself, I know this is wrong, but I do it for you.

Chapter Eleven

When we got home it was eight o'clock, breakfast time. And there was pandemonium in the house.

Aunt Hannah was in the dining room, shrieking. "No," she was yelling, "don't."

We ran into the room to find Walking Breeze about to set a hot pan down on the linen-covered table.

"I cook for you," she said. She was smiling.

Then the hot pan was set down on the table.

You could *smell* the scorched wood and table linen. And whatever was *in* the pan stank like it had been dead for three days.

Uncle Louis ran into the room, grabbed the handle of the pan, burned his hand, and without complaint reached for a napkin to hold it.

"My table!" Aunt Hannah's hands went to the side of her face. "It's ruined." She sank back in her chair, sobbing.

"I'm sorry, Hannah," Uncle Louis said.

Cecie came in with some old rags. Uncle Louis

set the pan down on them. "I'll buy you a new table."

"I don't want a new one. This one was my mother's!"

"The child doesn't understand about tables," he said. "Come, Hannah, becalm yourself. You're frightening her. I'll have the table *repaired* for you." His tone had a pleading in it.

Walking Breeze was retreating toward the kitchen.

"Sit." Uncle Louis turned to her. "We thank you for your food. Sit with us, please."

But she just stood there, arms folded across her middle, head bowed.

"Food?" Aunt Hannah asked. "Are you saying this is *food*?" Clearly, she was distraught. True Salem lady that she was, she took great pride and comfort in her commodious home and its furnishings.

"It's hominy cooked with cattail roots," Uncle Louis explained. "Indians eat this when they have no game. She made it for you, Hannah. She likes to cook."

"Louis," Aunt Hannah said, "you don't expect me to eat it, do you?"

"It is not polite to refuse."

Aunt Hannah looked horrified. "Louis," she whispered, "I cannot eat that." Then, to Walking Breeze she said, "We have food. See?" And she walked to the sideboard where breakfast was laid out on silver platters.

"You have given me to eat," Walking Breeze said softly, "so now I give to you. I am very much sorry that I hurt the table." And she started to creep back to the kitchen.

"No, Walking Breeze." In a few swift strides, Uncle Louis was beside her and had one of her hands in his. "No," he said again. "Aunt Hannah wants you at the table with her. Hannah!" He turned. "You must make her feel welcome."

"I did that last night, Louis. We all did. I will *not* eat that . . . *food*. Don't ask me to." She went back to her place at the table and sat down.

"I'm not asking you to eat it, Hannah," he said gently. "I am asking you to speak to the child. Tell her, 'I lift you up from this place and set you down again at my dwelling place.' "

Aunt Hannah just stared at him as if he'd taken leave of his senses.

"It means that you invite her to come and live with you," Uncle Louis said. "Please, it's very important."

"Very well." Aunt Hannah sighed and repeated the words in slow, measured tones. I had to give her credit. In view of the ruined table, I think it was most gracious of her.

It worked like a charm. The girl allowed herself to be led to the table and sat down.

"Come sit, Ebie," Uncle Louis directed.

I sat.

"Now, let's start again," Uncle Louis said. "Let's everyone eat together. It is very important."

I could see the Indian agent coming out in him. And he was very good at it.

Aunt Hannah started to serve Walking Breeze eggs. The girl shook her head no.

"She won't eat eggs, Hannah," Uncle Louis said softly.

"Not eat eggs? Why?"

"She just won't. Don't expect her to. Or chicken or pork, for that matter. And she won't eat more than two meals a day. The Shawnee consider that sufficient. Of course, if she gets hungry in between, she will expect to be able to eat whenever she wants." Having made this speech, Uncle Louis commenced eating. He ate the awful-smelling stuff as if he were accustomed to it.

Aunt Hannah glared at him and I felt some stirrings of hope. What had I been worried about? All Walking Breeze had to do was be herself, and she would soon have the whole household in an uproar. It had started already.

Now the girl sat eating some fish and bread. "You don't eat what I cook?" she asked Aunt Hannah sadly.

"I have poor digestion," Aunt Hannah lied.

"It's very good, Walking Breeze," Uncle Louis said. "Where did you get the cattails?"

"Behind the place where the horses are."

"Behind the barn, yes. And you cooked this outside, then?"

"Yes. I make a hole in the ground. And a fire. I put the pan in the ashes."

Aunt Hannah's cup clattered into her saucer. *"You made a fire in my garden?"* She was out of her chair like a shot.

We followed. She stood at the back door of the kitchen, hands covering her mouth. "My garden!" The words were strangled.

Whether there were greater sins in the world was up for conjecture at that moment. The sight of the upturned earth, the ruined bushes, the smoking ashes was too much for Aunt Hannah.

She whirled on Walking Breeze. "You dug up my currant bushes and my white rose bush! Would you do this to your mother's flowers?"

Walking Breeze started to reply, then decided not to. Instead, she turned and ran through the kitchen, the hall, and up the stairs.

"Hannah!" Uncle Louis said. "Now look."

"No, Louis, *you* look. Look at my garden!"

"They don't grow flowers, Hannah. They grow beans, corn, squash, and some other vegetables. Flowers have no meaning for her, except as they thrive in the wild."

"Well, if she's going to live here, she's going to have to understand about things like flowers and tables."

They stood glaring at each other. I watched, delighted.

"The frost will soon kill the bushes," Uncle Louis said.

"That isn't the *point*, Louis."

"I know the point, Hannah." He sighed and

ran his hand through his dark hair. His thin face was lined with distress. "Look, I am asking you to be patient. There are bound to be some mishaps like this. It's difficult enough for her to have to sit on stick chairs and eat strange food, without you being angry with her."

"*Stick chairs?* Louis, those are Chippendale. So is the table!"

I wished I could take notes. Mary would love this.

"I know what they are, Hannah, in heaven's name." Uncle Louis minded Cecie watching them then, put a hand under Aunt Hannah's elbow and gently guided her back into the dining room. I followed.

"I'll ask John Gardener to set all the damage in the garden to rights," he said soothingly. "I am sorry, dear girl. And if you can find a man to fix the table, I'll pay for it. Now there are other things we must speak of. Before I leave."

"You're leaving? When?"

It was exactly the effect he wanted. He pulled out her chair at the dining room table. She sat down. He poured coffee for her and himself. He had forgotten I was even there.

"Mayhap tonight."

"Why?"

"Because I must return. I've a meeting with Harrison. And we must talk, Hannah, before I go, you and I."

"I have school. Elizabeth, so do you."

"No school, Aunt Hannah," I reminded her. "It's Training Day."

"Well, my mill children don't have a holiday. They must work. You know, Louis, that I and some other women see that they get a nourishing noon meal. I fought for that with my father. And for a few precious hours every day to instruct them." She was talking very fast, avoiding his eyes.

He put his hands over hers on the table. "Hannah," he said tenderly. That was all.

It was enough. She stopped her chatter and met his eyes then, and she must have seen some terrible truth in them. A truth she did not want to see.

"Very well, Louis. I'll be home at one," she said quietly.

"Thank you, Hannah." He stood up. "I have business to attend to. I'll be back later."

He left. And we sat looking at each other across the ruined Chippendale table.

I felt the ending of something, but I did not know what. I think she did, too.

"Well. I behaved badly, didn't I?"

"No, Aunt Hannah. I think you were most gracious. Considering everything that happened."

"I was not gracious. The shock of meeting the girl. I dreamed all night. Of Thankful."

I did not speak.

"How did Georgie behave toward her father?"

"She didn't, Aunt Hannah."

"Oh, dear. Poor Louis. How awful it must have been for him. And then to come back to this."

She gestured to the table, the ruined breakfast, everything. "Well, I must try to make it up to him. And to the girl. But I just can't think of her as Thankful's daughter, Ebie. I was up half the night trying."

Again I remained silent.

"I must get the table repaired before my father gets home. Are you going with Aunt Mattie to see the Salem cadets in their new uniforms?"

"I'm going to Mary's. She has a book of plays by Voltaire."

"Very well, someone may as well enjoy the day."

I left the table. Uncle Louis was going to tell her, this afternoon, that he knew Aunt Thankful was alive all these years.

I wished I could be around to hear it. Perhaps Mary and I could come back here. Yes, I would invite her for tea. Aunt Hannah always liked it when I was gracious.

Chapter Twelve

I spent the morning with Mary, in her room. I told her everything. I sat on the floor while she sat at a small desk, writing in her journal.

"What will you do with all that writing?" I asked.

"I will have it published someday."

"Aunt Hannah says women are hard put to get published in this country."

"Then I'll keep it for my grandchildren. By then they'll be publishing women in this country."

"How will you get grandchildren, if you're never going to give your heart to a man?"

She sighed deeply. "Do you always have to make things so difficult, Ebie?"

"I wouldn't keep a journal. People might read it, like I read Aunt Hannah's."

"I keep my journal well hidden."

"Suppose you die. Moses might find it."

"I shall destroy it before I die."

"Then how can your grandchildren publish it? And what's the profit in keeping it at all, Mary?"

"Ebie," she explained patiently, "if sea captains can keep ships' logs, I can keep this record of my life's voyage."

I decided there was something lacking in me. I did not have the need to record my life's voyage. Most of the time, I had trouble just keeping afloat. "Let's go to my house and have tea," I said. "It's baking day. Cecie started early. She's already done the breads and is working on the cake."

"Man cannot live on bread alone," Mary said. "Nor can woman. But even I am not above being tempted by fresh cake."

I had been right. At home, Aunt Hannah and Uncle Louis were having high words behind the doors of Grandfather's study.

I left Mary in the kitchen with Cecie. Walking Breeze was in there, elbow-deep in flour. She'd been helping Cecie with the baking all day. I slipped into the hall. Mary was fascinated with Walking Breeze and nobody would miss me for a few minutes.

"You're angry with me, then," I heard Uncle Louis saying.

"And why shouldn't I be?" Aunt Hannah's voice was shrill. "For *twenty-two* years you allowed us to think she was dead!"

"What could you have done, had you known she was alive, Hannah?"

"Dear God, how do I know? If I'd known she was alive, I might have had some peace of mind.

— 103 —

To say nothing of how such knowledge would have affected my father and brother."

"She was happy, Hannah. It's the reason I stopped going to visit her. She needed no more reminders of the past. Do you think your father would have allowed that? He'd have had the secretary of war lead a raiding party on that village!"

"You could have told *me*, Louis. I thought there was trust between us."

Trust was a very big commodity with Aunt Hannah. She once told me she'd spent most of her life acquiring it.

"I trusted you to raise my daughter, didn't I?" Uncle Louis's voice was raspy with feeling.

"I failed miserably with that. And you know it. And now you leave me with still another half-Indian girl to care for."

Silence for a moment, terrible, stretching, tearing silence.

"You forget something, Hannah."

"Then I can depend on you to remind me."

"This one says she is your sister's daughter."

"It's so difficult for me to think of her as such. Why didn't you leave well enough alone? Why bring this girl back now and raise our hopes? Suppose she *isn't* Thankful's daughter. All you've done is opened old wounds."

"She told me she had proof, Hannah."

"And you never asked her for it?"

"She said it would be as smoke to me. But to you it would be like fire."

"In heaven's name, Louis, speak English."

"It was important to her that I take her on her word. I've often had to do that with Indians and found their word good. Would you rather I *didn't* take her word? And left Thankful's daughter out there?"

"Well, why doesn't she bring forth this proof now?"

"She told me the time must be right. It's the way of them, Hannah. They are patient people."

"Well, I'm not."

I heard her sniffling.

"Don't let the lie I told you about Thankful turn you against her daughter," he said.

In the quiet that followed, I knew he was kissing her. Then she said something. It sounded like, "You tie me to you once again with this girl."

I heard his answer. "I tie you no more. I free you."

That made her cry.

"Too much talk disgraces a man and is fit only for a woman," he said.

"Dear God, Louis, you've been living out there too long. You talk like one of them." Her voice was brighter.

"I must go now, Hannah. I'll be wanting to speak to the girl before I leave."

"Oh, Louis!" Her voice broke.

Then another silence. This one longer. When it was over, I heard his boots striding toward the double doors. I moved quickly. I ran back into the kitchen.

"Ebie, Louis would like to see you outside before he leaves." John Gardener came into the kitchen with that message.

Uncle Louis had gone into the back garden with Walking Breeze. From the window as Mary and I fetched our tea, I could see him talking with her. Then John brought his horse out of the barn, all saddled. And Uncle Louis led it around to the front of the house.

I went through the hall and out the front door. He stood waiting at the gate, fussing with the stirrups.

"I hope you have a safe trip, Uncle Louis," I said.

"You were wrong, Elizabeth." He did not look up.

"Wrong?"

"Yes." He flung his saddlebags over the horse's rump and secured them. "Your aunt Hannah couldn't abide the telling."

He did look at me then. And he was stone serious.

"I thought she could."

"Well, I suppose I've been in the wilderness too long. I have the feeling that you spoke to me with your lips and not your heart."

"I don't take your meaning, Uncle Louis."

"Ponder on it a bit. You will."

The skies were darkening. The wind had picked up. Would it storm? None of that seemed to concern him. I did.

"When will you be back?" I asked, for lack of anything better to say.

"Likely never. You won't have to concern yourself with me anymore. Your aunt is free to marry Richard Lander."

I may have blushed, I don't know. I said nothing.

"Matter of fact, she always was, Ebie." It was not said in anger, but in sadness.

"I'm sorry if I was wrong, Uncle Louis," I said. He was going away. I could afford to be generous. "If there's anything I can do for you, sir."

He stood with one hand holding the reins, looking at me. "I believe you are sorry, Elizabeth. And there is something you can do for me."

He stood as if studying on the matter. "Do you know what broken days are?" he asked.

Broken days? It sounded sad. "No, sir."

"It is the way the Indians speak of the length of time set for the completion of some task. I don't know how many broken days Walking Breeze has given herself to convince your family of who she is. But you can count on it, she's given herself a certain amount of time."

I nodded. He went on.

"Indians don't shilly-shally. They get to a task

and do it. And they don't take forever. Do you understand?"

"I think so."

"And they don't beg anyone for anything, either. When her broken days are up, Walking Breeze will stop trying to convince anybody of who she is."

"What will she do then?"

"I wouldn't want to see it go that far, Elizabeth. It would be bad for all concerned."

It was starting to rain, lightly. I looked at him in his frontier clothing. His words carried the weight of a way of life I could never understand. But the man was striking. And you had to pay him mind.

"It's not easy growing up in your family. I think you can attest to that. Can't you, Elizabeth?"

I nodded yes.

"So can Georgie. It's too late for her. But I'm asking you to be a friend to Walking Breeze. She's going to need it."

"Yes, sir."

He gave me a long look. Aunt Hannah was right. He had been living with the Indians too long. He not only spoke like one, he could see into your soul, as I imagined Indians could.

Then he mounted his horse. The animal's forelegs moved swiftly, prancing. He reined it in, steadying it, and gave me one more look, filled with meaning. Then he put pressure to the horse's flanks. The last thing he did was take off his hat and nod to me as he rode away.

For the first time in my recollection, Aunt Hannah did not preside at the supper table.

The rain turned into a proper New England storm. It beat against the windows. Wind rattled the shutters. John Gardener went about tending the fires. Candles flickered. Cecie fixed a tray for Aunt Hannah and bade me take it to her room.

Walking Breeze had made Marlborough pie. I'd seen her, struggling to learn, earlier in the kitchen, refusing to understand when Cecie said the apples had to be peeled. I felt a stab of resentment, though the pie didn't look like much. I could see the apples were soggy.

Aunt Hannah was propped against lace-edged pillows, looking every bit the languishing heartsick maiden in her high-necked nightgown. I was surprised to see the portrait of Uncle Louis already hanging in her room. "Where is the girl?" she asked.

"In her room."

"You made Marlborough pie? Wherever did you get the time?"

"Walking Breeze made it. She's been helping Cecie in the kitchen all day."

"Louis said she loved cooking."

"Yes. But I don't think she likes Cecie's rules."

Aunt Hannah sniffed. Then she brought herself about. "So the girl likes to cook, does she? Well, that could be an answer. For now. Until we find out who she truly is. I'll put her in Cecie's charge. Do you think that would be awful of me?"

"Cecie seems taken with her, Aunt Hannah. But it's going to take a lot of patience for her to learn our ways."

"I can't send her to school. We don't know how the community will receive her. And she certainly won't accommodate herself to its habits. Look what she did to my table. And my garden."

"John Gardener is having the table fixed," I said.

"I heard she slept on her mattress on the floor. Is that true?"

"Yes, Aunt Hannah."

"Dear God." And she sighed. "I tell you, I see Georgie all over again. And I am *not* going to allow this girl to do to me what Georgie has done. I will not give her my heart and have it destroyed." Her words were full of passion.

"I must first find out if she is really my sister's daughter. You must help me, Ebie."

"How?"

"Louis says she has proof of who she is. Has she made mention of it to you?"

"No, ma'am." The lie came easily. I didn't feel bad about it, either. I minded that it was probably what Aunt Hannah wanted to hear.

"This girl has nothing of Thankful about her. Every child has something of his parents. You have your mother's laugh, Ebie."

I flushed with pleasure. Oh, I knew what Aunt Hannah was doing. My family always did it when they wanted a favor from me. They spoke of my mother. Though I knew what they were about, it always worked for me, like throwing a bone to a hungry dog.

"I think this girl has your uncle Louis bamboozled. Men are easy to bamboozle. Louis says we must win her trust before she offers her proof to us. Try to win her trust, Ebie."

"How?"

She studied on it a moment. "Parson Bentley is coming on Saturday. He wants to take you on a boat trip to sight the sea serpent. Perhaps you could invite Walking Breeze along. The parson is so good with young people."

But what if Parson Bentley won her trust? For a moment I felt panic. She would tell him about the quilt.

But if the quilt couldn't be found, who would believe her?

"I'll do it, Aunt Hannah," I said.

"Good. You're such a comfort to me. I shall have nothing but good to tell your father about you when he returns."

I kissed her and walked to the door.

"Ebie?"

"Yes, Aunt Hannah?"

"Her Marlborough pie can't measure up to yours."

I went downstairs. Cecie said Walking Breeze

Chapter Thirteen

"Where is your moon lodge?"

She was huddled in a buffalo robe on the mattress on the floor. In the fire's glow her face looked drawn.

"Moon lodge?"

"In my village, when a woman is in the time of her bleeding moon, she takes a bundle of clothing and goes to a lodge, away from the others."

I understood then. "We don't bandy such talk about here."

"And why? It only means I am a woman now. And old enough to bear children."

"We just don't. And we have no moon lodge."

"Then where do you go to be away from others?"

"We don't go away from others. Why should we?"

Her eyes grew large. "Others are permitted to be in your presence? To look upon you? You are allowed to prepare food for others?"

I said yes to all of it. "But we don't go around talking about it, either."

She nodded her head slowly. "Then you go into a moon lodge of your own making."

"What?"

"You would keep this thing a secret from everyone else. We are the same in different ways."

I didn't see it that way at all. But I did not argue the point. I set the tray of food down.

She sipped the soup quickly. She seemed starved. Then she ate the bread and cheese. "Are you old enough to bear children?" she asked.

I was taken back. "That is my own business."

She held up a small pouch with a drawstring. "I would know so I can give this to you, for in the time when you do not go to a moon lodge."

"What is it?"

"It takes away the drums in the head and the drawing down pains. It is made of roots and herbs."

I made no move to accept the pouch. She smiled to herself. "Hannah and Mr. Louis have big fight," she said. "With my people, we do not fight. Fighting is for dogs and beasts."

I nodded, listening. She was intent upon insulting me. But I must not allow her to know I was ruffled.

"White people always work against each other and cut what comes between them. They are like scissors. It is so with the British and the Shemanese. Only what comes between *them* is us."

She set her bowl of soup aside and looked around the room. "You have many pretty things here. Do you have many thieves in Salem?"

"Thieves?"

"You lock your doors."

"That isn't the reason we lock our doors," I said.

"Why, then?"

But I had no other reason to give her.

She nodded, wisely. "Why do the Shemanese set aside so much? You lay up stores. You cannot carry such treasures into the world of spirits. We will find all our wants met when we arrive there."

"Many of these things were given to Aunt Hannah by Uncle Richard," I explained. "He travels the world in his ships. He's in prison now, in England. The land owned by the British. My father went to get him out of prison."

"Where is your mother? Did she make the journey to the world of spirits? Like mine?"

"No. My mother and father are divorced."

"Di-vor-ced? What means that?"

I felt uneasy. "They don't live together anymore."

"Oh." A smile appeared on her face. "I thought it was serious bad."

"It is. You don't take my meaning."

"Yes. Walking Breeze understands. This is something many Indians do. Tecumseh himself has made this di-vor-ced!"

"Tecumseh?"

"Yes. Two years before I was born, Tecumseh moved the Kispokotha sept of the Shawnees to a new place in O-hi-o. My mother and father went with him. So did many other Shawnee septs. He became a great new chief and took a wife. Her name was Monetohse. They had a son. But she was not a good wife to Tecumseh. She did not take proper care of the boy. She scolded Tecumseh most of the time and made complaining noises. So he put her away from him and gave the boy to his sister."

I stared at her. It was what my father had done, too.

"This is an old Shawnee custom. We do not live together in marriage any more time than one is pleased with the other. This is not serious bad business, this di-vor-ced."

"It is in Salem," I said.

She shrugged. "Shemanese make big fires out of little sparks. Everyone in my village was happy for Tecumseh when he did this. He soon took another wife. She died when she birthed his second son. His name is Nay-tha-way-nah, a Panther Seizing Its Prey. I call him Cat Pouncing and he is my friend."

I took all this in silently. The fire gave good warmth and I was getting drowsy. Her words lulled me. A fierce rain was still splashing at the windows and I thought of Uncle Louis, riding off in it.

She smiled at me. "You would keep from me if you are old enough to bear children. But I think you are. It is not polite to refuse a present when it is offered to you."

She spoke of the pouch. And I saw my chance. "Parson Bentley has invited me on a boat ride to

Marblehead Bay," I said. "I will take the pouch, if you come with us."

She scowled. "Mr. Louis said I should not leave this place. He said the people of your village can be mean and bad."

"Parson Bentley isn't mean or bad. He's a reverend."

"Re-ver-end?"

"A man of God."

Her eyes widened. "A holy man?" She drew in her breath and shook her head. "No, no, I do not wish to meet him."

"Why?"

"I do not trust holy men. The one we had in our village was evil."

"The one who sent you away?"

"Yes."

"What else did he do to you? Why do you fear him so?"

Tears came to her eyes. "I cannot say. I have not yet cleared the path that leads from you to me."

I reached out and took the pouch. "If I take this will that help clear it?"

She smiled through her tears. "It is a beginning," she said.

Then I had a thought. "You like to cook, don't you?"

"Yes. But I do not know the Shemanese ways. I am afraid to offend Aunt Hannah."

"Well, would you come with me on the boat

trip if I promised to ask Aunt Hannah to allow you to spend your days in the kitchen with Cecie? Learning to cook like the Shemanese?"

"You would speak those words to Aunt Hannah for me?"

"Yes. You will be able to cook. Even in the time of your bleeding moon."

Her face became wreathed in smiles. I was almost ashamed of my deception.

"It is not polite to refuse such an invitation," she said. "I will go with you on this boat."

Chapter Fourteen

By the time Parson Bentley came on Saturday, Walking Breeze had spent two days in the kitchen, cooking with Cecie.

She learned how to prepare salt fish with cream, bean porridge, cider soup, boiled pork, and cabbage. She was tireless in her apprenticeship. But she made no more Marlborough pies.

She got up at first light and stayed most of the day in the kitchen, taking special delight in tending the small beds of glowing coals in the oven, learning how to put her hands inside and feel the bricks to test the warmth. And where to place the footed pots and skillets in the hearth.

Cecie had always wanted to teach me these things. I never wanted to learn. Now Cecie walked about full of importance. The way people get when others seek out their talents.

Walking Breeze even ate in the kitchen with Cecie. All this upset Aunt Mattie very much. "You can't let her be a *servant*, Hannah," she said.

"No one is a servant if they do something by

their own choosing," Aunt Hannah said.

But Aunt Mattie knew better. When she and Uncle Richard were young and poor, she had once been a servant girl in this house, before she married Uncle Lawrence. "A serving girl is still a serving girl," she said. "Whether she wants to be one or not."

"So this is the newcomer to the family," Parson Bentley said. "It is good to meet you, my dear."

I could see him studying her, looking for signs of Aunt Thankful, whom he'd known as a young girl. And I could see, too, that he found none.

Walking Breeze became flustered under his scrutiny. She made a poor curtsy. "I must go and help Cecie." And she ran from the room.

I'd seen Cecie teaching her to curtsy in the kitchen, instructing her how to pick up the corner of my old dress. She can't curtsy, I'd thought watching. But she filled out the dress better than I ever had. And I was green with envy.

Parson Bentley turned to Aunt Hannah, smiling. "A pretty child," he said.

"Do you see anything of Thankful?" Aunt Hannah asked.

"No, Hannah. But it has been years. Don't judge her by that. Now I have news. A clergyman friend writes from England that Richard has been taken to Dartmoor Prison."

"Dartmoor? Richard?" Aunt Hannah seemed

confused and agitated. "What manner of place is this?"

"It's on the Devonshire moor, north of Plymouth. It houses thousands of French prisoners from the Napoleonic wars."

"Has your clergyman friend seen him?"

"Yes. He is well. And will be writing soon."

"How will my father find him if he is moved?" I asked.

The parson smiled at me. "Your father's friend, Mr. Burnaby, is very influential in Parliament."

"Can I write to Uncle Richard at Dartmoor?"

"Yes, child, do," he said, "write soon. Now get the girl from the kitchen and let's be off. The sea serpent awaits!"

Cecie was instructing Walking Breeze in the kitchen on how not to attract attention as an Indian when she went out. Cecie spent hours instructing her, it seemed. "And what English name have you chosen for yourself?" Cecie asked.

"Today I shall be Nancy," Walking Breeze said.

Cecie helped her into Aunt Hannah's old but good woolen cloak. She wore it over my old striped dress. But she *would* attract attention, I minded. There is something about an Indian girl dressed in the clothing of whites that makes everyone take notice.

Because such a sight points out our similarities? Or our differences? I have not yet decided. But the results are always striking. Yet a new name could make Walking Breeze no different.

She would not speak to us on the ride to the wharf. She shrank back from the warm greeting of Captain Hathaway. She was in terror of the noise and confusion of the harbor, the stares of the workmen and sailors.

Parson Bentley was gallant and protective with her. Still, on the boat she found a place to cower by some coiled rope.

Parson Bentley and I stood at the railing watching the harbor recede in the background.

"Has she never been on a boat before?" he asked me.

"Likely not. But it isn't the boat that frightens her. It's you." And I told him of the holy man in her village who had done something to hurt her.

"It will take time for me to win her trust," he said.

The boat ride was lovely and I was determined to enjoy it. As we entered Marblehead Bay we opened the picnic basket Aunt Hannah had sent with us. But Walking Breeze still would not join us, or take our food.

As we stood near the railing eating our bread and cheese, one of the hands shouted "Ahoy," and pointed. "The sea serpent. Off the starboard bow!"

We ran to look. For a moment we saw nothing. Then the parson pointed. "There it is!"

I looked in the direction in which he pointed. Then I sighted it, dipping up and down, in and out of the water. It seemed to be part of the water.

"One, two, three, four," Parson Bentley was counting. "It's got twenty protuberances on its back! It's as Captain Hogkins saw in Ipswich Bay! There is the head, three to five feet! Like that of a seal!"

I stared in disbelief. Oh, how I wished Mary could be here, but she and Moses had taken their parents to see family in Boston. Oh, every time the long, green-gray creature surfaced above the water, I felt a new sense of fear and a thrill of excitement. My eyes followed it desperately, not wanting to lose sight of it. "Oh!" I jumped up and down. "Oh, I see it, I do!"

"Aye, we've all seen it, and I'll vouch for it," said Captain Hathaway.

Parson Bentley was hastily scribbling notes. He planned to write an account for the *Essex Register*. "This is the same serpent who appeared in Kettle Cove fifty years ago! And it's the fourth time he's been seen in the bay of late. We must take him! He has made us a laughingstock in southern states. They say we conjure him from the air. They accuse us of conducting a witch hunt against a whale!"

I saw Walking Breeze pick her head up. She looked puzzled. She knew nothing of whales or witch hunts. Nothing of the lore of New England or the sea.

"We must determine what kind of creature he is and why he is visiting our harbors!" the parson was saying.

"Do you not know a sign when it is given to you?"

The girl had come to stand behind us, clutching her cloak.

"A sign?" the parson asked.

She raised her dark eyes to his face. "You claim to be a holy man. In my language we call a sign of good fortune *unsoma*."

"This is good fortune, then?" he asked.

She shook her head. "No, but this serpent has not come to harm you. He has come to warn you of things to be in your waters in time to come."

"What things?" the parson asked.

"Did you not say the serpent had visited here before?"

He nodded. "Kettle Cove. Fifty years ago."

"What trouble came in these waters then?"

Parson Bentley ruminated for a moment. "The year was 1761. From across the waters came the Writs of Assistance from the British. They allowed customs officers to enter and search anybody's house at will. It was the start of the trouble that led to our Revolution."

Walking Breeze nodded. "You Shemanese have much big trouble now with the British, do you not?"

"Yes. They have been seizing our ships for years. For a while they hovered near all our ports, just outside the three-mile limit. That was before President Jefferson's embargo in 1807."

"Did this em-bar-go help?"

"It near ruined our shipping. And the British still seize our ships and take our men prisoner."

The girl fastened her brown gaze on the horizon. "They will be back again in these waters," she said. "This is what the serpent has come to tell you. Do not kill this big fish. It is sacred."

"Thank you, Walking Breeze," Parson Bentley said. "But how do you come by such powers?"

"I have no powers. I just know how to read the signs Our Mother the Earth sends us. You white people do not respect Our Mother the Earth. You tear her bosom and destroy her heart."

The parson nodded solemnly. "I thank you for your help," he said.

She awarded him a smile. Then her confidence went out of her, like wind out of the sails. She drew her cloak tighter, and shrank away from him and went to sit on the rope. She did not speak another word to us all the way home.

Chapter Fifteen

End of October 1811

Dear Benjamin: I take pen in hand to write and tell you that I saw the sea serpent. Parson Bentley took me on a boat ride to Marblehead Bay and we sighted it.

Oh, Benjamin, it was so exciting! It was dipping up and down out of the water and the parson counted twenty protuberances on its back! It was the same creature seen by Captain Hogkins in Ipswich Bay. And Parson Bentley is writing an account for the Essex Register.

In accordance with our wager, you must now bring me a gift. I suppose you should keep it seemly and proper, like a book of poetry. But I wouldn't be adverse to a copy of Mary Wollstonecraft's A Vindication of the Rights of Women. I know you can get it in Boston. Of course, it is absolutely frowned on here in Salem.

Have you enlisted in the Boston militia yet? War is coming. It's all Uncle Lawrence talks about. He's near to distraction readying his troops for any need that arises.

Being that you owe me a gift, it is an excellent reason for you to visit. I have had no letter from you and therefore was not going to write. But Parson Bentley said I should. I suppose you are very busy and important in your uncle's counting-house. Have you made friends in Boston? I know there are many fine shops there and likely many fine ladies, too. Have you made new friends and forgotten me?

Do you recollect how you took me skating on the pond at Winter Island? And bought me three-cent cakes on Election Day? And all the times we went to Gallows Hill on the fifth of November? I suppose we are both too old now for such childish pleasure, but I look back on them with fondness, nevertheless.

Mary sends her warmest regards. Aunt Hannah sends her best, too. She says I am languishing over you. To set the record straight, I am not. I would not know how to languish and I know you'd laugh at me if I did. But if Aunt Hannah wants to think such, I do not wish to stop her. I need the air of secrecy such suspicions bestow.

You and I know we are just fast friends, Benjamin. We also know such friends are difficult to replace. So please write. I look forward to the favor of your reply in the near future.

Your dear friend, Elizabeth.

Dear Uncle Richard: I miss you very much and hope they will not detain you at Dartmoor too long. Aunt Hannah's concern for you grows daily. But she was cheered the other day by a letter from my father, saying his friend in Parliament is working diligently to have you released.

I know Aunt Hannah has written to you of Uncle Louis's visit and the Indian girl. I write that Uncle Louis is still very dashing. But I was viligant in looking out for your interests. He has left now and told me personally that he is not coming back. They are expecting trouble on the frontier with the Indians.

As for the Indian girl, well, she has the whole house in turmoil. She refuses to eat with us. She sleeps on the floor in her room and scorched Aunt Hannah's table with an evil concoction she made in a cast iron pot. From that moment on, everything she did only made things more onerous. And endeared her less to Aunt Hannah.

She has relegated herself to cooking in the kitchen with Cecie. Aunt Mattie and Uncle Lawrence think Aunt Hannah is making a servant of her. But she is in the kitchen by her own choice. She enjoys it. She does so much baking that Cecie is required to heat the baking oven every day now instead of once a week. Aunt Hannah is worried that such regular use will damage the bricks.

Then one day Walking Breeze decided to please Aunt Hannah by lighting the first fire of fall in our new Rittenhouse stove in the back parlor. Being Indian, Walking Breeze prides herself on knowing about fires. But she put in too much wood and the result was that we ended up with scorched woodwork, and smoke damage so bad that the back parlor had to be painted all over again.

The matter of the straw mattress was another disaster. As you know, Aunt Hannah has Cecie replace the straw mattresses with feather-filled ones every fall. Well, Walking Breeze became distraught when Cecie emptied out the straw from her mattress to wash the ticking. Next thing we knew she had slashed the feather-filled mattress, to see what was inside.

We looked out the windows to see feathers flying all over the backyard. It was like snow! And Walking Breeze was kneeling on the ground, stuffing pine boughs into the feather bed ticking instead. She cut these pine boughs off the beautiful trees that border Aunt Hannah's garden.

Aunt Hannah had to be put to bed with tea laced with something a bit stronger. Cecie defends Walking Breeze. "Whose side are you on?" Aunt Hannah asks her.

Cecie says, "I didn't know there were sides." But there are, and she does know. Our house is becoming like a divided camp.

Uncle Lawrence says he doesn't have to go to war. He has it right here. And mayhap he ought to bring in some militia to keep order.

Aunt Hannah is muddled in her feelings about the girl. Aunt Mattie feels so guilty seeing her in the kitchen that she has taken to tutoring her in letters and sums. You know what a dear soul your sister is. But it seems that she is falling under the Indian girl's influence.

One day Aunt Mattie asked Uncle Lawrence how he could let his militia march against the Indians. "This poor dear child's people have suffered because of what we have done to them," she said.

Uncle Lawrence explained that it wasn't his militia, that it was under the jurisdiction of Governor Strong. And that no one was sure yet whether it was constitutional for the militia to respond to such a call, since we were not being invaded.

"You mean you would refuse the president his militia?" Aunt Mattie asked. Uncle Lawrence said he didn't know what he meant. That he'd already had many a sleepless night over it, because the governor was depending on him for advice. And that he wasn't apt to know with that Indian girl in our midst, looking at him with her big brown eyes.

Walking Breeze has Uncle Lawrence completely undone. He runs to melancholy in her presence. Aunt Mattie says the girl is a constant reminder to him of how he lost his little sister in the West.

Only last week I heard Uncle Lawrence telling Aunt Hannah to please try to find out what proof the girl has that she is family. That having her amongst us is only causing mayhem. And we are a family ill-equipped to negotiate with mayhem.

As for proof, Uncle Richard, I have seen it. And it was meager at best. A scrap of quilting made mostly of animal pelts. I think the girl brought it from her village, yes, but that she acquired it somehow after Aunt Thankful died. I do not think Aunt Thankful was her mother.

She died only recently. She was alive all these years. Uncle Louis told us that on his visit. He'd known it all along, but kept it secret. Of course, he couldn't tell us if this girl is Aunt Thankful's daughter. He hadn't seen Aunt Thankful in years.

None of this sat well with Aunt Hannah, especially finding out her sister was alive all these years, I can tell you. She says she sees none of her sister in this girl. Neither does Parson Bentley.

As for the quilting — the proof — the girl wasn't about to bring it forth. I think she was afraid of being discovered as a fraud. So I stepped in. I got rid of the quilting.

To my way of thinking, Aunt Hannah doesn't need to be led into thinking this girl is family, then disappointed. I don't think she could abide it. I think she would lose her senses. And I think it was cruel of Uncle Louis to bring this girl to us, without first determining who she really is.

I know you will understand that I acted for us all. Besides, war is coming. The Indians are aligning themselves with the British. There have been remarks directed at Aunt Hannah already, because we have another half-Indian girl in the house. To my way of thinking, the sooner she is gone the better. We all need some peace in this family.

Please don't tell my father any of this. You always said I could confide in you and you would honor my secrets.

Well, that is all the news for now. Except that, with all the rest, we now have a sea serpent in our harbors. Parson Bentley took me and Walking Breeze on a boat, and we saw it. Walking Breeze says it is a sign, a warning that soon British ships will be in our waters again. Sometimes she gets very otherworldly. But Uncle Lawrence says all Indians are that way.

I have, however, promised to be nice to her. By now I have promised so many people so many things, that I fear I can never remember my promises. I know I cannot make good on them. But as part of this promise, Mary Palmer and I are taking her to Gallows Hill for the bonfires on November fifth.

I pray for your quick return. Please try to keep. I can't wait for you to come back and make Aunt Hannah happy again. She needs you, Uncle Richard. So do we all.

Your affectionate niece, Ebie.

Chapter Sixteen

November 5, 1811

"The least you could do is stay in on my last evening home, Mary," Moses Palmer said.

He stood on the Palmers' front steps, glowering. His brig, *Lydia*, was to have cleared Salem Harbor on the fourth. But a storm that blew all along our coast on November third delayed his departure. He was not in a good frame of mind.

"I stayed in Tuesday evening. It's no fault of mine you couldn't sail," Mary said.

She'd just dashed out of the house to stand beside me and Walking Breeze. We were all dressed like Indians for the festivities. It was the evening of the fifth and we were anxious to get started.

"The public mind is at unrest, Mary. Many little wharves below Crowninshield's were damaged in the storm. People are arguing on street corners about the war. They are looking for a scapegoat."

"Don't try to frighten me," Mary said.

But he kept at it. "Look at how someone had to rescue that poor pig who ran about with his head half cut off last night."

"That was done by Andrew Poole," I volunteered. "They told us in school today. He's always been deranged."

Moses set his eyes upon me, nodded, and gave a half-bow. Then he did the same to Walking Breeze. Apparently he did not realize who she was.

"Dressed like Indians," he said. "The three of you are courting trouble."

"All the young people will be in disguise," Mary reminded him. "You did it once yourself, Moses."

He mumbled something about it having significance when he was young. Now it was naught but silly superstition.

"You speak of superstition?" Mary laughed. "You who say the *Lydia* speaks to you?"

"Of course she does. All ships do. If the master is sharp enough to listen." Then another thought seized him.

"John Proctor died yesterday in Boston," he said. "His ancestor was hanged for a witch. Earlier this week some people digging in the earth around the old Phillip English house found a large glass bottle with his name on it. He and his wife were thrown in jail for witchcraft. There are those who would make much of such events this night."

Mary and I looked at each other in delight. "Such news adds spice to the festivities," she said.

"Be home early, Mary. Or answer to me."

She giggled and we walked off. "You've angered him," I said.

"Moses is an old bear without claws," she assured me. "He's sour as bad milk because his sailing was delayed. He wants to be off, yet dreads leaving because my brother Josiah's ship hasn't returned yet. I must let him play at being the surly older brother. He feels he must act the part."

"And watch that Indian girl," Moses called after us. "You are responsible for her this night, Mary. Hear me."

"I hear," Mary called back.

So, I thought, *Moses had known all along who Walking Breeze was. And he'd bowed to her as he had to me. I had new respect for the man.*

I envied Mary for having a brother. For I felt that he was doing more than playing. I felt he really cared for her.

The fires on Gallows Hill were under way when we arrived. And people were coming forth out of the night, greeting one another. I heard snatches of conversation.

". . . aye, the pig had its throat cut with a saw."

"They say the boy used the saw in his daily labors, when his mind and body did allow him to do such."

". . . Terrible, such wanton violence. And from one of our own! What's become of our young people?"

". . . Look, someone has the bottle with Phillip English's name on it."

". . . and look, there's an image of John Proctor!"

Walking Breeze was taken with the whole scene. "Once when he was young," she recounted, "Tecumseh watched a white prisoner being burned at the stake. It was then that he told the other warriors he would never again take part in such torture. Why did you burn the witches?"

"We didn't," Mary said, "we hanged them."

"Hanging is better?" the girl asked.

Mary laughed. "No."

"Then why make great fires to celebrate the hangings?"

Our ways came hard to her. Often I heard her badgering Aunt Mattie with whys in her tutoring sessions. And sometimes it seemed like her questions made more sense than Aunt Mattie's answers.

"They help us to remember," I told her. "But also, this is the last time we will gather outside before winter comes. Winter is hard in Salem. Sometimes the harbor freezes. Or a sailor falls from a ship's icy rigging. Some of the poor freeze in their houses. Or children fall through icy ponds and drown."

"Like the starving time that winter means to us," she said.

"Well," I said, "yes." And now it was I who didn't understand. "See?" I pointed. "They are roasting apples and three-cent cake. Let's get some."

We feasted on hot cider and three-cent cakes. The fires' orange glow cast great shadows. Young people said hello to us and we did not recognize them for their disguises. Some were dressed as Puritans, some as Indians, some as witches.

Above us on Gallows Hill the old hanging tree loomed. People said it was not the same tree from which the witches were hanged. But nobody cared about that. Selectmen stood under it, talking. The Salem militia did their best to keep people a safe distance from the fires. But every so often, a young boy would break through the militia line and throw a log on the flames.

"They are very brave," Walking Breeze said of the boys.

"They are a nuisance," Mary said.

Then out of the dark reaches of the night came the Salem cadets up the hill, fifing and drumming for all they were worth. The drumming, with its sense of purpose, sounded in my bones.

Walking Breeze went rigid with fear.

"It's all right," I whispered. "It's only sport."

She nodded, but kept her eyes on the soldiers.

I think everything would have been all right if the cannon hadn't gone off then.

"Shemanese cannon!" She gripped my arm.

"It's only the Salem artillery," Mary told her. "See there? Up on the hill."

But the girl was terrified. And Mary and I were hard put to becalm her. Then, of a sudden, she ran.

"Walking Breeze!" I yelled. And then I froze in my tracks. She was running toward a figure who stood out in her Indian garb. No costume, this dress was made of soft deerskin, beaded and fringed. The woman also wore leggings and a silver band on her head. Her hair was done neatly in braids.

I gasped. It *was* Georgie. "Mary, look!"

Mary grabbed my arm. "She looks *beautiful*. Where did she get those clothes?"

Georgie did look beautiful. It was the first time I had seen her looking anything but slovenly in years. "Likely from her trip west. But beautiful or not, Mary, Walking Breeze is following her. We can't let them meet. Hurry!"

We ran. We pushed our way through the crowd. Then the Salem artillery fired their cannon again and smoke settled over everyone. And we couldn't see. For a while we groped about. It was terrible. I felt fear-quickened. *We had lost Walking Breeze.*

We searched for the next half hour. We fell once on the ground, already slippery with frost. We asked dozens of people if they'd seen a young girl dressed as an Indian. They laughed and pointed all around them.

I started to cry. My heart raced, my head started to pound. "What will we *do*, Mary? She'll never find her way home. Aunt Hannah will never forgive me."

"Georgie will get her home," Mary said.

"That's even worse. That those two should meet."

We must have walked up and down Gallows

Hill five times. I was footsore in the soft moccasins. Finally, as the whole celebration was ending and people were starting home, Mary looked at me.

"There's no profit in wandering around in the dark, Ebie."

"I can't go home without her."

"I think we must. I think we should get help."

She was right, of course. Only stragglers were left on the hill, unsavory types, who were giving us sidelong glances. We left.

We trudged home disconsolately. At every turn, every shadow, Mary put a hand on my arm and we'd peer, hoping to find Walking Breeze. But always, we were disappointed. We hurried down Main Street, past shuttered shops and private dwellings. Our only beacons were the whale oil lamps spilling their light out of fancy houses with pilastered doorways.

It was that time of night when darkness swirls in, all mixed with the mist, harboring sea smells that are dank and ominous in content and give rise to our basest fears. No human who has his senses is out on the streets at this hour.

Finally we crossed over onto Derby Street. As we came close to my house, Walking Breeze was there, standing on the front steps, as if waiting.

I ran to her. "Where *were* you? Why did you leave us?"

"I have spoken with one of my own." She smiled at me serenely. "Why did you not tell me she was here?"

"She isn't one of your own," I lashed out. "She's no Indian."

"She is part Shawnee, as I am," the girl insisted.

"She is also part lunatic," I countered.

Mary tried to hush me. But I would not be hushed.

"You'll be in serious bad trouble with Aunt Hannah if she finds out about this," I warned.

But Walking Breeze would not be bullied. "This Geor-gie has invited me to visit her," she said simply. "She is *dah-nai-tha* to Mr. Louis. Daughter."

"No! Walking Breeze, I mean it. I forbid you to visit her." I reached out to grab her, to shake her if necessary.

"Ebie, don't." Mary interceded, holding me back.

"I knew I shouldn't have taken you tonight," I flung at Walking Breeze. "I was trying to be nice. Because I made a stupid promise to everyone that I would be nice to you. Well, I shouldn't have bothered."

"And you kept your promise," Mary said, "consider the virtue of that."

The only virtue I considered was that I didn't hit Walking Breeze then and there. I was fixing to. The way she stood and smiled, all serene and superior-like, afflicted me so, that I probably would have hit her if Moses hadn't come along then.

"Mary, is that you up there? What's the trouble?" He came out of the darkness, lantern light spilling before him. "What's amiss, Mary? I was worried. You should have been home by now." He threw a warm cloak around her shoulders.

"Nothing's amiss, Moses. I was just saying good night to Ebie."

He looked at the three of us and nodded politely to me and Walking Breeze. But I know he saw my tearstained face and had heard the loud words. Yet all he said was, "Go inside, you two, your folks will be worried."

We went up the steps. Just before I went inside, I heard what he said. "Good news, Mary. Josiah's ship has been sighted off Naugus Head. He'll be in tomorrow. I feel a sight better leaving now. You and the old folks won't be without a man's protection."

He had his hand on her shoulder. For the second time that day, I envied Mary. I would have given anything to have a brother to come up searching for me in the dark night. Mary had four of them. It wasn't fair.

Chapter Seventeen

November 6, 1811

The next morning Walking Breeze was gone. When Cecie came into the dining room and announced, "Miss Hannah, I can't find my Nancy," I suppose I should have expected it.

"What do you mean, you can't find her?" Aunt Hannah asked.

Cecie said what she meant, right out. "She's gone."

"Gone where? Where would she go?" Aunt Hannah was not prepared for this. The older I got the more I realized that she lived in a nice little orderly world of her own making. And when something went amiss, she could not abide it.

"She didn't come to the kitchen to put the bread in the oven this morning." To Cecie, this in itself meant disaster. Walking Breeze had been doing this all fall.

Right off, Aunt Hannah looked at me. "What do you know of this, Ebie?"

"Me?" I looked indignant.

"What happened last evening? John Gardener

said he heard upraised voices out front when you came home."

There was nothing for it but to tell her. "She ran from us on Gallows Hill. She met Georgie."

Aunt Hannah closed her eyes. "Dear God," she murmured, "give me strength. Dear God, why have you visited such trouble on me? What have I done?"

When she was finished addressing the Deity, she addressed me. "Do you think she went to Georgie's this morning, then?"

I thought so, yes. "I told her you wouldn't like her going there," I put in. "But she doesn't listen."

"Very well. You must bring her home then. You will not go to school this morning. Finish eating, then go get her."

"But I have watercolor lessons this morning!" I loved my art lessons. "Why should I be punished, Aunt Hannah? I've done everything to get the girl to trust us."

She minded then, that she was being unjust. "It's an emergency, dear." And she sighed. "So please help me one more time. I shall send a note around to Mrs. Peabody, and you will make up your watercolor lesson."

"We should send for Lawrence," Aunt Mattie said.

"It isn't that much of an emergency," Aunt Hannah said.

"Then I shall go with Ebie." Aunt Mattie got to her feet. "Walking Breeze is my pupil, after all.

I feel a sense of responsibility. Come, Ebie, we'll be on our way."

The day was cold, without sun. A brisk breeze off the harbor made it colder. The one tree in front of Twenty-one Union Street was etched bare over the sad little house. We knocked on the front door.

No answer. From inside I heard Octavius, "Spaniards on deck. Spaniards on deck. Look lively!"

"They're in back, cooking."

We turned to see little Nathaniel Hathorne peeking around the corner.

I thanked him and we went around back. There they sat, huddled in blankets. Ragged smoke rose between them over a hissing fire. Walking Breeze was chanting something in a low and steady voice. Georgie was smoking her long pipe. The Prophet was curled up beside her.

It was a nightmare seeing them together. One reason being that this house was where the piece of quilt was. I heard Aunt Mattie take in her breath. Likely it was a nightmare for all of us. It was as if our haunted past and our uncertain future met here in this ragged little backyard in the bleak November cold. And it was dressed as an Indian.

"Walking Breeze, you must come home," I said.

She kept on chanting.

"Walking Breeze!" I shouted her name.

She stopped. "With our people only one speaks at a time. Others wait and listen until the speaker is finished."

"I'm not waiting. You must come now. Aunt Hannah is distressed that you are here."

"It is no surprise that you Shemanese cannot understand one another when you all speak at once." And she began chanting again.

"She is praying," Georgie said, "for the success of Tecumseh and our people in coming battles."

"You are both smoking the weed that makes your heads muddled," I accused. "I smell it." A cold gust of wind had blown the stink of the weed my way.

"It is *nilu famu*, the sacred tobacco," Georgie said. "I gave some to Walking Breeze."

Before I could belabor the point, I noticed smoke on the ground in front of me. Apparently that cold gust of wind had blown ashes on dried leaves and started them burning.

The small fire spread quickly, even while I stared at it. I tried to stamp it out with my feet, but then the hem of my cloak caught and got scorched. And the smell of burning wool filled my nostrils.

"Do something!" I yelled at Georgie. But her eyes were riveted on Walking Breeze, who was still chanting. It flashed across my mind that the two of them were in some other place with their chanting, that they wouldn't have moved if half of Salem were burning down.

"Be still!" Aunt Mattie was beside me, reaching

for the ties of my cloak. I tried to stand still while she undid them and pulled the cloak off me, then began beating at the burning ground with it.

The fire was gaining, all around us, greedy flames licking at the dried leaves, the grass turning black. Then a small figure came running toward us with a bucket. Little Nathaniel Hathorne, struggling with his burden, came dashing over. "Here," he offered.

"Thank you." Aunt Mattie threw some water on the ground around me, dousing the flames. The fire hissed and gave up steam. My shoes got wet. Then Aunt Mattie threw the rest of the water on the fire between Georgie and Walking Breeze.

They scrambled up. Their fire sizzled and went out. "You have killed the sacred fire!" Walking Breeze shouted. "Now Tecumseh and my people will be in danger!" But her voice was slurred and her eyes glazed.

I was too shaken to respond. I was shivering, what with my wet feet and my anger and fear.

Aunt Mattie took off her own warm cloak and put it around me. She was white with rage. Her round, pleasant face was honed in anger. She looked like Uncle Richard when he got angry, with her blue eyes blazing and her bottom lip thrust out. "Sacred fire, indeed! Georgie, how could you give this child that terrible weed to smoke? It's rendered her silly and irresponsible. Otherwise she never would have made such a mistake with fire.

Don't you know what a terror everyone in Salem has of it?"

Georgie stood implacable, puffing her pipe.

"Stop smoking that pipe," Aunt Mattie scolded. "What's in it has made you both senseless!"

"You've no right to walk in here and tell me what to do," Georgie said.

"I've every right! I can have you arrested for smoking in the streets. It's against the law!"

"I'm in no street, but on my own property."

That fine distinction was lost on Aunt Mattie. "Suppose the fire had burned Ebie? Or spread to this little boy's house? No, Georgie, you are wrong."

"You put out the sacred fire." Walking Breeze could not get beyond that fact. To her it was incomprehensible. "Do you not know what you have *done*? Now my people are in grave danger."

"Stuff and nonsense," Aunt Mattie said briskly. "It's all silly superstition."

Walking Breeze had tears in her eyes. "What do you know of the ways of my people? I have been to your meeting house with Hannah. I do not say that the ways of your holy men are silly, though they look like starving crows, all dressed in black."

Aunt Mattie was taken back. I saw her blue eyes blink with understanding. "I apologize, Walking Breeze," she said solemnly. "I do not mock your customs. But Georgie is not a good influence. We want you to come home."

"She is Shawnee. So am I."

Aunt Mattie sighed and again I saw Uncle Richard, the way he must look on the foredeck when there was an abrupt change in weather and he could not see anything within twenty yards ahead.

"We're going home," she said. To Aunt Mattie that was the answer to everything. She was bringing in her ship.

"Nathaniel," she said and she turned to the boy, "thank you for your help. You are a dear child and I shall send a note to your mother telling her so."

"My grandfather Hathorne fought at Lexington," the boy said. "He was a minuteman. Mama says I have a lot to live up to."

"Indeed, you do," Aunt Mattie agreed. "And how is your mama faring these days?"

"She's doing as well as can be expected."

"You come round to our house on your way home from school. Ebie will have cake and cider for you."

He ran off, delighted.

"Now, Walking Breeze, must I send Ebie for my husband, to get you home?"

The girl laughed. "Your husband prays in his decision making. Like a woman."

"My husband," Aunt Mattie said, "was just commencing to listen to my arguments against sending his militia to invade Canada and fight against your people."

The girl's eyes went wide. "He listens to advice from his woman? White men do this?"

"My husband always listens to me. I am not saying he will do what I ask. But if you refuse to mind, I shall speak no longer against his militia invading Canada."

The girl knew when she was beaten. "I must go," she told Georgie. "Mr. Lawrence is big in the hearts of the Shemanese walking soldiers."

Georgie scoffed. "Mr. Lawrence will arm his soldiers against our people, and don't be fooled into thinking otherwise."

Walking Breeze looked at her. "Tecumseh often stops his ears from hearing what his warriors have to say. But he always listens to his sister."

My heart was fair to bursting with love for Aunt Mattie as we left. "It was like having Uncle Richard here," I told her.

"I pray he comes home to us soon, Ebie," she said.

As we walked from the backyard I saw two of Georgie's cats curled up on the back porch. They were snuggled on the piece of quilt I had brought over.

Aunt Mattie had one arm around each of us. "To tell you the truth, Walking Breeze," she was saying, "our clergymen do look like starved crows in all that black clothing."

Chapter Eighteen

It was our milkman, Mr. Purkitt, who told Aunt Hannah, even before we arrived home, about the chanting of Indian songs and the fire. Mr. Purkitt doesn't miss much.

"He upholds a tradition of communication in Salem that goes back to the Revolution," Aunt Hannah told us, "when our Committee of Correspondence knew everything going on in Boston practically before General Gage did."

She spoke with bitter irony. She had, I might add, changed from her morning gown to her dark blue dress. She was not about to be trifled with.

"Walking Breeze," she said as we came into the parlor, "you claim to have proof of who you are?"

The girl nodded.

"Then fetch it. Now."

Walking Breeze backed away. "But the time of the broken days is not yet finished."

"Broken days?" Aunt Hannah asked.

"It is the time we set to finish a task. I need

more time. I must still clear the path between us."

Clearly, Aunt Hannah had had more than enough. "The path is as clear as it will ever be, Walking Breeze. Go fetch your proof. We will wait here."

The girl left. We sat down to wait. Aunt Hannah took my cloak from Aunt Mattie and sat down to cut off the burned edges. She worked with a vengeance. "Likely Mr. Purkitt has the story through half the town by now. Haven't we had enough with Georgie? I cannot allow these two to join forces. I must put a stop to it."

Aunt Mattie made me take off my wet shoes and warm my feet by the fire. She was more somber than I'd ever seen her. The extent of damage to my cloak made her shudder.

Cecie brought tea. "Is my Nancy in trouble?" she asked as she served it.

"I fear she is," Aunt Hannah allowed. But she would say no more. Cecie left and we heard a lot of banging around in the kitchen. We waited. I sipped my tea. From the street came the sound of carriages, then the conch shell of the fishmonger from about a block away.

"Ebie," Aunt Hannah directed, "get a pair of moccasins from the hall and catch the fishman." She reached into her reticule on the table for some money. "Get some fresh cod for supper."

I rushed to do her bidding, anxious to be out of the room. I needed to think. I slipped the moccasins on in the hall, ran to the kitchen for a bucket, then back through the hall. My thoughts scrambled.

This morning's events had reaffirmed for Aunt Hannah the possibility of another Georgie in Walking Breeze. She could not bear it. If the girl was not who she said she was, she must do something about it now.

And, my last thought: Walking Breeze was upstairs looking for a quilt that did not exist.

Some women had come out of their houses to gather around Mr. Phinney, the fishmonger. I waited my turn.

"Haddock in great plenty," he said. "No cod."

"Three pounds of haddock," I said when my turn came. Aunt Hannah liked extra.

"Everyone keepin' at your house?"

"Yes, thank you." I paid him.

He eyed me warily with a rheumy gaze that had seen much in sixty-some years. "Heard 'bout the doin's of the Indian girl this mornin'. Tell your aunt she has my sympathy."

I ran back into our yard. But I would tell Aunt Hannah no such thing. His sympathy was the last thing she needed.

"Hold your aunt in great esteem," he yelled after me. "Wouldn't want to see no more trouble. You're all good people."

I thanked him and ran into the house and dumped the pail with the haddock in it down on the table, right in front of Cecie. She glared at me, but said nothing.

Walking Breeze was standing in the middle of the parlor.

"What do you mean, *gone?*" Aunt Hannah was asking her. I minded it was the second time this day she'd asked the question.

"It has been spirited away," the girl said.

"What was this proof?" Aunt Hannah asked.

"A piece of quilt. It was with my mother when she was taken. From her time here in Mass-a-chus-etts."

Aunt Hannah gasped. Her hand flew to her heart. *"You claim to have a piece of the quilt that my sister took west?"*

"I do not know what means this claim. I speak the truth."

Aunt Hannah had to sit down. Her knees seemed to buckle. "What did it look like?"

"There were many fine animal skins in it," Walking Breeze told her.

"Animal skins?" Aunt Hannah was confused.

"Yes. And a piece of buckskin from my father's shirt. And a bit from Star Watcher's dress."

"Star Watcher?"

"She is *Neeshematha* to Tecumseh. Sister. And there was a bit of cloth from something I wore as a baby. Also some from a hunting shirt of Cat Pouncing's. And best of all, there was a bit of deerskin from the leggings of Tecumseh's."

Aunt Hannah looked beaten. Aunt Mattie took

up for her. "Were there other pieces of fabric in this quilting?"

"Some. But they were old and faded."

"But why didn't you give it to me when you first *arrived!*" Aunt Hannah was near crazy by now.

"It was not the time," Walking Breeze said.

"Oh, don't give me any more nonsense about broken days!" Aunt Hannah got up and began to pace. "Where would the quilt have disappeared to?"

"I do not know," Walking Breeze said. "I put it in the place with my other things. Ebie told me to put it there."

"Ebie, have you seen it?" Aunt Hannah asked.

So there it was, then. It lay with me. Dreadful silence in the room. I could hear the wind outside, the blowing of the conch shell of the fishmonger down the street now.

I looked at my aunts. For all their years and wisdom, they were innocent. I had to protect them. I had to protect all of us.

"I helped her put her things away in the chest of drawers," I said. "It was late. We were both tired. Mayhap she thought the quilt was there. I did not see it."

I heard the intake of Walking Breeze's breath. Then a soft moan.

I was surprised at the ease with which the lie rolled off my tongue. Surprised that the good Lord did not strike me dead on the spot. I did not have any special religious fervor. But I had been raised with a good Puritan conscience. I knew lying and deception were wrong. But I also knew of other wrongs that had taken root and flourished in our house. And I was determined to lie for the rest of my born days if it would keep such wrongs from taking root and flourishing again.

"Or mayhap the quilt never got here," Aunt Hannah said.

Walking Breeze raised her eyes to meet Aunt Hannah's. "Do not listen to the singing of this little bird," she begged.

"And why not?" Aunt Hannah asked. "Why would Ebie lie?"

"She does not wish to give me room to spread my blanket in this place."

"Nonsense," Aunt Hannah said briskly. "Ebie has been most kind to you. She invited you on a boat trip. She took you to Gallows Hill."

"She does not want me here!" Walking Breeze cried.

"We all want you here, Walking Breeze," Aunt Mattie said, "if you are who you say you are. But Mr. Louis only brought you because you said you could prove it."

"Did you deceive Mr. Louis in saying you had proof?" Aunt Hannah's voice had dropped to a whisper.

"I spoke good words to him, Miss Hannah."

Aunt Hannah turned away, sighing. "If you did indeed have such proof it would warm my heart more than you could think, Walking Breeze," she said sadly. "I would welcome you with open arms as Thankful's daughter."

The girl was not stupid. "And now?" she asked. "The path between us is choked with briars, then?"

Aunt Hannah nodded. "I am sorry, Walking Breeze."

"Then what is to become of me?" the girl asked.

"I don't know," Aunt Hannah said. "I hadn't thought of it. But now I suppose I must." She looked at Aunt Mattie, who nodded at her in encouragement. "You may continue to live in our house. You are a great help to Cecie."

"I will be no slave to the Shemanese," the girl said bitterly.

This struck Aunt Hannah and hurt her. "No, of course not. I will pay you for your service. Until we can come up with another plan. Or until the quilting is found."

"And I will continue to tutor you," Aunt Mattie said. "So you are versed in your sums and letters. And perhaps you can get a position elsewhere."

"I will work for my keep," Walking Breeze agreed. Then she started out of the room. At the door she stopped and turned. "Until I can find another place to spread my blanket." Then she fled.

"Well," Aunt Mattie said, "this is a fine kettle of cod."

"Haddock," I said.

"What?" she looked at me.

"There was no cod," I told them. "Mr. Phinney only had haddock. In great plenty."

Aunt Mattie tried to control her laughter, but couldn't. It burst from her. Of course, I started giggling. I had felt myself near to a rising panic all along.

Aunt Hannah followed, laughing, too. Then, of a sudden, she commenced to cry. Aunt Mattie put her arms around her and started crying, too.

I joined in. And we clung to one another. "Don't cry," I told them. "We're good people."

"Are we?" Aunt Mattie asked. "Will we be judged as such?"

"Yes," I said.

"Oh, Ebie, child, how can you know?" Aunt Hannah asked.

So I told them. "Mr. Phinney, the fishmonger, said so."

Chapter Nineteen

End of November 1811

After that, matters settled down in our house. If you want to consider Cecie's cold silence, Aunt Hannah's nerves, and Aunt Mattie's sighing because Walking Breeze was now truly a servant as things settling down.

Uncle Lawrence didn't help, either. He tried to say cheerful things to Walking Breeze when she served us at the table, but she would not look at him. This threw him into a fit of melancholy. He did not know what to do about it. To add to it all, I heard him whisper to Aunt Mattie that the only thing keeping the town fathers from complaining about the fire at Twenty-one Union Street was the damage from the recent storm.

Then toward the end of the week, Aunt Hannah smiled at me at breakfast.

"The Crowninshields' *Fame* dropped anchor late last evening. Very early this morning its captain sent word. Your grandfather will be home for Thanksgiving."

You would think that she and her father were

devoted. They were not. They were sworn adversaries who had learned over the years to respect each other. In some ways this made the bond between them tighter.

Thanksgiving is our foremost holiday. We in New England celebrate family, hard work, independence, and our self-righteousness about the fact that we do not keep Christmas.

Aunt Hannah knew all about Christmas from Aunt Abby's letters. "It smacks of popery," she once told me, "and we'll have naught to do with it."

I always thought that, with its balls and assemblies, its roasted geese and chestnuts and evergreen boughs in the house, Christmas sounded rather nice. But we made up for it with our Thanksgiving.

Every night, in the two weeks before the holiday, Aunt Hannah dragged me to market at eight in the evening, after all the ships had been unloaded. Of course, dragged isn't the proper word, for I always loved going to market.

We purchased nutmeg, Virginia corn, Irish butter, German chocolate, Mocha coffee, loafed sugar and our turkeys, beef, cider, raisins, cranberries, and hyson-souchong tea.

Farmers came from the country and crowded Essex Street, from Central to Washington. And an air of festivity reigned.

We were invited to two Thanksgiving frolics, one at the Crowninshields' and the other at the

Peabodys'. But Aunt Hannah declined. She would rather have a quiet Thanksgiving at home, with family. She had invited Parson Bentley, Aunt Mattie and Uncle Lawrence, Mary and her parents and brother Josiah.

But I knew Aunt Hannah could not even consider going to a frolic when Uncle Richard was starving in prison.

A week before Thanksgiving, Uncle Lawrence came to our house with a letter from Uncle Richard.

With a quavering voice and tears in her eyes, Aunt Hannah read some parts to us. " 'We have an allowance of only half a pound of peas and one and a half pounds of bread a day. But I am surviving,' " the letter read.

By now a freezing room in our garret was piled high with vegetables that gleamed like jewels, breads wrapped in linen napkins, and pies.

"Hannah," Uncle Lawrence said gravely, "I have other news. Not good, I'm afraid. Word at the wharves has it that a storm blew father's ship off course. He may not be here for the holiday."

Aunt Hannah clutched Uncle Richard's letter to her bosom and she and Uncle Lawrence looked at each other. "You mean he could be lost at sea?" she asked.

Uncle Lawrence gave a short, bitter laugh. "Not likely," he said.

I knew what he meant. And I felt gratified

because I could understand one of my elders for a change. Grandfather loomed, second-in-command only to God as far as his position in the community and his power over all our lives. Uncle Lawrence had grown up under that power.

The sea would not dare.

But Aunt Hannah's gaze was stricken. "We will give extra this year to the poor," she said.

It was the custom on the night before Thanksgiving for children to don shabby clothing and go door to door, begging. Mary and I had done it and loved every minute of it. Normally, Aunt Hannah did not hold with this tradition. And this year, thinking of Uncle Richard starving, she had assembled stockpiles of food for the poor with a vengeance.

The night before the holiday, she stationed me and Mary at the back door. Inside the kitchen were bags of Indian meal, sacks of apples, and rice and flour, containers of tea and sugar, raisins and, of course, chickens.

"It's for the poor," she told us sternly. "Don't let me hear that you've given it away to any costumed children."

We promised. But we were hard put to keep that promise. When the sound of small feet rustling through fallen leaves came to us out of the dark and the cold, one of us would sneak some apples or raisins or maple sugar candy out of the house, while the other stood watch.

We'd put a finger to our lips. We'd douse the light. We'd urge them to run. The children, of course, delighted in the air of secrecy.

"Food, food, please, I'm starving," one little child said, holding out his pillowcase.

He was dressed as ragged as any I'd seen this night. "I'm a widow. I've seven children to feed," he said.

I recognized the voice of Nathaniel Hathorne. "Keep him hidden," I urged Mary. "I'll run upstairs and get a pie."

My breath was nearly wasted by the time I came back down. I put one of my Marlborough pies in the pillowcase.

"Oh, my favorite." And he ran off into the night.

It was the least I could do, I thought, for the lonely little boy who had brought the bucket of water that may have saved me from serious burns.

Grandfather returned in the middle of the night the first week in December. We knew that afternoon that his ship was sighted off Naugus Head, but I was not allowed to wait up.

The minute he was in the house, I knew it. It was as if a hand was put on my shoulder to rouse me from my deep sleep. I lay in the dark and it seemed that the texture of the night itself had changed as I heard his voice in the hall outside my room.

"How *are* you, Father," I heard Aunt Hannah ask.

"I'm terrible. It was a nightmare of a voyage. Our vessel was thrown on her beam ends three times. We were blown off course four times."

He said something else. Then words that pulled me fully awake. "I heard at the wharf, Hannah, that on the seventh of last month, Governor Harrison attacked and defeated Tecumseh's Indian settlement. The news just arrived and everyone was overjoyed. They are calling it the Battle of Tippecanoe."

As I lay there, all I could think of was the fire we'd extinguished at Twenty-one Union Street. It had been on the sixth of November! Again, I heard Walking Breeze's words:

"You have killed the sacred fire! Now Tecumseh and my people will be in danger!" I heard the words as I went back to sleep.

The first gray fingers of light were reaching into my room when I awoke. I had been dreaming. Walking Breeze was chanting her primitive song.

But when I opened my eyes the chanting did not stop. It sounded like it was coming from the back of the house. I got up, threw on a robe, and went into the hall to peer out the window.

There in the cold December mists knelt Walking Breeze, over a small fire. She was dressed in full Indian garb.

"Great ghost of Caesar, what is that?" From his

room at the end of the hall, Grandfather strode out.

I was surprised to see how old he'd gotten. He was thinner and his shoulders were more stooped. His hair was nearly all white now, as was his beard. Both had streaks of red. But after a few moments I saw how none of that mattered. His presence was as domineering as ever.

So was his voice. It boomed. "Who is that benighted fool out there chanting like an Indian?" He came to the window. I stepped aside.

"It's Walking Breeze." Aunt Hannah came up behind him. "It's the girl who claims to be your granddaughter. I wrote to you of her, Father."

"You mean *this* is the one? She looks like an Indian squaw."

"She dresses that way sometimes," Aunt Hannah said weakly. "She claims to be Thankful's daughter."

"I don't care if she claims to be George Washington's daughter! We can't have her carry on like she's some daft Mohican out there. Especially now, Hannah, with sentiment in town against the Indians as it is."

I spoke up then, though I don't know why. I may have felt the need to speak, to make him look at me, acknowledge me. "She isn't a Mohican. She's a Shawnee," I said.

He glared at me. "Eh? What's the difference?"

I cringed, feeling unworthy. He had always done that to me. "Well, sir, I don't rightly know. But

I do know that she's burning a sacred fire for Tecumseh and her people."

"Sacred fire?"

"Yes, sir." I started to tremble. The house was ungodly cold.

"Hannah, do you hear what this child is saying? It's downright heathen! This is a good Congregationalist household! Is this the kind of goingson you've permitted in my absence?"

"I have done everything I could to try to civilize the girl, Father," Aunt Hannah said. Then she turned to me. "Ebie, go down and bring her into the house."

I saw the despair in Aunt Hannah's eyes. And I ran.

"Father, go back to bed," I heard her saying. "The house is chilled."

"How can I sleep now? I want my breakfast."

Aunt Hannah said very well, she would summon Cecie. Grandfather grumbled. "Public sentiment whipped up against the Indians! And what have I got! Right in my own house? I won't have it, I tell you, I just won't have it."

Chapter Twenty

December 1811

That morning at breakfast, it started. Aunt Mattie, who always came to our house for breakfast, was waiting for me in the hall.

"Don't be upset," she told me, "it always happens when he returns from a trip. He must re-establish himself as the master of the house. So he must test your aunt Hannah's mettle. For the next few days, they'll argue about everything. Just for the sake of argument. If he says the sky is blue, she'll say it's green. Then they'll settle in."

We went into the dining room together and took our places at the table.

"That's a rather harsh decision, don't you think, Father?" Aunt Hannah was saying.

"I'm a harsh man."

"I've noted that."

"She'll have a room, what more does she want?"

"The lean-to off the kitchen is in disrepair. And freezing in winter."

"Then have John Gardener repair it. No servant shall occupy Abby's room."

I stared at Aunt Mattie. *He was going to put Walking Breeze in the kitchen lean-to.* She scowled at me and shook her head.

"You've spoken ill of Abby for twenty-two years," Aunt Hannah argued. "You've discouraged her from coming home. And now you treat her room as a shrine."

He was reading the *Salem Gazette.* He shook it out in impatience. "You think I wouldn't be the first to embrace this girl if she was Thankful's daughter? She is *not* Thankful's daughter. I had a conversation with her before breakfast. And I know it."

"How?" Aunt Hannah asked. "Because she does not have one blue eye and one green? I wish you would tell us, Father. We are all in a state of guilt over her."

"You may be in a state of guilt, but I am not," he said. "I know it because my girl would never make the choice to stay with the Indians and not come home to me." His voice trembled.

No one said anything. No one dared.

"As for the lean-to, she won't be there for long. I have plans for her," he said.

"Plans?" Aunt Hannah's voice cracked.

"Yes. I shall put her in the mill. Mr. Lowell and I are working on our Grand Design and plan to open the mill in Waltham soon. Once that happens, she will live with other mill girls in a respectable boarding house."

Aunt Mattie spoke up now. In horror. "You

can't put her in the mill," she said.

"And why not?" He smiled at her. It had something of the wolf in it.

"Why, she's unlettered!" Aunt Mattie said. "Isn't that the problem you had with young girls in your mill last time?"

He scowled. "This time it will be different," he said. "This time we will hire only educated girls from good farm families. And we'll offer them more education and culture. We'll have lectures for them. Our town has much culture to offer."

"But Walking Breeze scarcely knows her letters and sums," Aunt Mattie persisted.

"You've been tutoring her. Step up the process. Or don't you feel capable of it?"

Aunt Mattie flushed.

Aunt Hannah's anger flared. "Mattie has done a wonderful job! But Walking Breeze prefers cooking to learning. She would be an asset to one of Salem's leading families. She loves mixing and stirring, brewing and making things."

Grandfather's eyes narrowed. "Then I'll have her learn dyeing. We will be dyeing as well as weaving in our mill."

"Dyeing is an art," Aunt Hannah said. "The only woman I know who does it well is Sarah Bryant." The moment she said it, I could see she was sorry.

Grandfather smiled again. And the wolf turned into a jackal. "Write to your friend. Ask her to take Walking Breeze this winter and teach her to card, weave, and dye."

"She won't do it," Aunt Hannah said quickly.

"Won't she? Why?"

Her face flushed. "Don't you remember? We sent Georgie. She ran away. It was the first time Sarah failed with a girl. I can't ask her to take another half-Indian girl."

Grandfather set his newspaper down. "Did I never tell you how I got her husband his first position as a doctor in Cummington in 1801?"

Aunt Hannah's face went from red to white.

"They were always moving," he went on. "Betimes they shared space with other families. Or lived in rented rooms. I heard that Cummington needed a doctor. I used my influence. I even found them the Snell farm."

"She won't do it," Aunt Hannah said again. But her voice was not so steadfast now.

"Write to her this morning." He stood up. "I leave for Boston tomorrow with Mr. Lowell to see our financial backers. Mattie, continue to tutor the girl. Hannah, have Cecie freshen and launder my clothes. Elizabeth, come to my library."

"Me?" I near dropped my fork.

"Your name is Elizabeth Chelmsford? Is it not?"

"Yessir."

"Then come along. Great Caesar's ghost, is everyone in this house addled?"

Chapter Twenty-one

Grandfather could be charming when it suited his purposes. And it suited his purposes now. He gestured that I should sit. Then he smiled at me. "Elizabeth, you are growing up."

I flushed. "Yessir."

"Remember, when you are sixteen, we are going to England together. How long before you will be sixteen?"

"A year and a half, Grandfather." I felt a surge of joy. He hadn't forgotten his promise. Oh, my father would be so happy.

"Good, good. Let's hope this dreadful threat of war will be removed from us by then. I must use all my energies to get the new mill under way before war comes, so we are no longer dependent on England for fabric."

My spirits fell. He didn't care about our trip. He was just saying what needed to be said to get him through the moment. Then he got to the real purpose of our meeting. "Your aunt told me this Walking Wind claims to have had a piece of quilt my Thankful was once working on."

"Walking Breeze, Grandfather."

"Hey?"

"Her name is Walking Breeze. Not Walking Wind."

"Does it make a difference?"

"Yes. Her name is important to her."

He nodded, as if he were truly giving the matter consideration. "Well, I'll tell you what is important to me, Elizabeth," he said softly. "And it's that we determine if this girl is an imposter or not. Can you understand how important that is to me?"

"Yessir. It's important to everyone."

"I want to give her every benefit. So then, your aunt Hannah said she is claiming you saw a piece of that quilt the night she arrived."

"I know what she told Aunt Hannah, sir."

"Well? And what have you to tell me of this, then?"

"There was no quilt."

I saw how this pleasured him. He smiled, and I saw the wolf again. "You never saw it?"

I did not wish to pleasure him. I felt at odds with myself for doing so. But I must stick to my story. "There was no quilt. I never saw it."

"I knew it! I knew it!" He stood up and commenced pacing. He slapped his open hand with his fist. "She is *not* Thankful's daughter! My girl would *never* have stayed with those people and refused to come home to me! Never did I hear anything so ridiculous!"

He stood, hands clasped behind him, looking down at me. He was filled with the joy of truth. The truth I had just given him with my lie. I had given him a gift of it. I could take it back any time I chose to. I felt a little bit like God must feel, I minded. When He gave us things and then took them away.

"Do you get on at all with this girl?" he asked.

"After a fashion, Grandfather."

"Well, I would like you to do me a favor, Elizabeth. I would like you to help her move from her room. I can't have her in that room, you know. A servant. It isn't seemly. I think, until the lean-to is fixed, she should move downstairs. In with Cecie. Will you help her move her things?"

I nodded. "I think you should tell her that Cecie will look out for her," I said. "Cecie will, you know."

Once again he slapped his palm with his fist. "That's it! You are a bright girl, Elizabeth. You have a little of the diplomat in you. Do you think you take after me? Just a bit?"

"I think mayhap I take after my father," I said.

He stared at me, then looked down at the papers on his desk. "Yes. Well, see to it." And in the next moment it was as if I did not exist for him. As if I had never existed at all.

I stood in the doorway of Aunt Abby's room and said Walking Breeze's name, softly.

She turned. A look of disdain crossed her face.

"I've come to help you move your things," I said.

"I want no help from one who has a viper in her breast."

I stepped into the room. "I'm sorry we put out your sacred fire. But I could have been burned."

"This battle that was lost was the fault of The Prophet. I grieve, because he has destroyed what Tecumseh built. But when Tecumseh returns, he will unite the people to destroy the Shemanese."

"My grandfather wants you to move in with Cecie. She will look out for you."

"I can make my own way, on my own path."

"Aunt Hannah has spoken with Cecie. She is clearing a place for your pallet in her room." I was surprised at how easily I had slipped into her way of speech.

"Your grandfather is a wicked man. And you have his blood in your veins. Or you would say true words about my quilt."

I did not reply.

She glared at me. "Go from me. You block the sun."

"Cecie has a nice room. And when John Gardener fixes up the lean-to, it will be lovely," I said stupidly.

"The poorest *wigewa* I ever lay my pallet in was better than the grandest room in this house," she said. "Now I know why my mother chose not to come home."

Her quiet words fell on me like cold rain.

She was folding her blanket. "Only you have the power to speak the words to tell this grandfather who I am. But now I do not know if I wish him to be my grandfather. The shamans in our village were more grandfather to me than he is."

I turned to go.

"You may have him to yourself, this grandfather who does not wish to be one. He told me he could not believe my mother would choose not to return to him. He cannot accept this. Because it injures his pride. Who could return to such a man as this?"

I ran my tongue along my lips and said nothing.

She gathered her bundles. "He does not even wish to be a grandfather to you. But your eyes are blinded when you look on him as if you looked on the sun."

I wanted to tell her she was wrong, that I saw him for what he was. But I could not speak.

"One day this sun will go black for you. And you will shrivel and die. I will not die. Because I have been raised to make my own sun. Here." And she tapped her chest. "Inside me. I was raised Shawnee. I do not need him. I do not need anybody."

I nodded.

"You little Shemanese girl, you need *everybody*. You were not raised to be strong."

I sighed. "He wanted me to tell you he will take care of you," I said.

"I work for my keep. You have delivered his

— 174 —

words. Now go from me. The council fire between us has gone out."

It was snowing lightly the second week in December when Aunt Hannah's friend, Sarah Bryant, came to fetch Walking Breeze. Outside our house a very fancy carriage was parked. A young man waited next to it. Aunt Mattie said he was Sarah Bryant's son, William Cullen Bryant. He looked bored and restless.

Sarah had gone upstairs to fetch Walking Breeze. At her request, Aunt Hannah waited below stairs with me and Aunt Mattie.

Aunt Mattie was at her wit's end, wringing her hands. Cecie was up there, too.

After what seemed like a Methodist eternity, they came down. Walking Breeze was dressed in a smart outfit, a dress of a striped design that I had never seen before. Over it she wore a rich-looking, warm cloak. Cecie was carrying her bags.

In the center hall, Walking Breeze hugged Cecie, who was crying quietly. Then she curtsied to Aunt Hannah. "Thank you for your hos-pi-tal-i-ty," she said.

Grandfather came out of the library and stood in the hall. He and Walking Breeze stood facing one another. You could hear the fire crackling in the parlor, it was so quiet.

He shook hands with Sarah Bryant. He inquired after her family. He thanked her for coming. Then he spoke to Walking Breeze.

"You have the best of teachers," he said. "Do not throw away this opportunity."

Walking Breeze stood very straight. She did not answer, but she nodded. I thought her eyes looked blacker, her skin more taut across her cheekbones and that, for all the swishing of the striped dress as she went out the door, she looked more Indian than she ever had before.

Chapter Twenty-two

Second Week of December 1811

Oddly, the house seemed empty without Walking Breeze. No more chatter came from the kitchen, no more happy banging of pots. And no more special dishes were made. Cecie cooked only what was required and seldom spoke to us.

Grandfather started traveling New England to see to his Grand Design. Thanksgiving was over. Winter loomed. Our house had an aura of gloom about it. And I was filled with guilt about Walking Breeze.

We hadn't heard from Uncle Richard or my father. I became afflicted in spirit. Christmas was coming, but we did not celebrate Christmas.

This year, however, Mary came up with a plan. I think it would have been construed as outright sedition if either her family or mine got wind of it.

"They are decorating St. Peter's Episcopal with greens," she whispered to me one day at school. "They smell heavenly, I hear. And the choir is practicing special music for Christmas. Let's sneak over there and smell the greens and listen."

The idea presented itself to me like a bright candle. But I knew that my upbringing dictated that I argue against it.

"Christmas is European superstition," I said. "Grandfather says it is the season that beguiles sensible men."

"Since we can't claim the distinction of being either sensible or men," Mary said, "why don't we go? Just once?"

We went. Right after school. It was snowing lightly. There was a dusting of snow on the ground. But outside the door of venerable old St. Peter's, I hesitated. "I've never been inside an Episcopal church," I said.

"Neither have I. That's what makes it such great sport."

"God may strike us dead."

"I think He has other things on His mind."

"Suppose they make us leave?"

"I don't think they do that. Anyway, we'll just stay in back. In the shadows. I hear there are lots of shadows."

"What if someone sees us and tells our families?"

She thought for a moment. "We can say we're studying history. This church was started by Phillip English, who was put in jail during the witch trials."

She thought of everything. We went inside.

It was damp and cold. Candles flickered. But in

a moment I became accustomed to the darkness, the candles, the shadows. Because Mary had been right. The choir was practicing. And the smell of evergreens was the most wondrous smell in the world.

"Mary," I whispered, "it smells better than Cecie's gingerbread."

"Listen to the music," she said. "It feeds the soul."

I had never heard Christmas music before. There was a majesty and hope about it that brought tears to my eyes and made me feel happy and humble all at the same time. As for the church itself, it gave off some dankness and mystery. It was connected to the past. I felt the spirit of Phillip English and others who had gone before him. If this was what the Episcopals were about, then we Congregationalists could learn from them.

"Do you think this is what heaven sounds like, Mary?"

She nodded. She had a rapt look on her face.

For at least ten minutes we stood and listened to that music and smelled those greens. When we left, we didn't have much to say to each other. We walked home in near silence. But the cold didn't seem so cold anymore. Or the leaden skies so leaden and unforgiving.

"You mustn't tell anyone," Mary cautioned when we got to my door. "It's our secret. To take to the grave."

I liked the idea of having a secret to take to the grave.

"And we'll do it next year, too," she said.

I went inside. God hadn't struck us dead. I felt something light inside me, as if I'd tapped into some wellspring of secret reassurance.

What we all need in this house is a little European superstition, I decided. And if this is the season that beguiles sensible men, then mayhap we all needed some beguiling.

The first week in January the flannel sheeting arrived in a package from Cummington, for Aunt Hannah. "I warpt a piece of flannel for Mr. Chelmsford's bed," the note from Walking Breeze said. "Yr. obedient servant."

Grandfather was delighted with the flannel sheeting. He had it put on his bed that very night. His delight made me jealous. Never had I done anything to earn such praise from him.

In February came another package. Table linen for Aunt Hannah. It was woven in a Damask pattern. Aunt Hannah was very taken with it. Grandfather was moved, near to tears. "I knew that girl could be taught," he said. "Sarah Bryant can teach anybody."

Aunt Hannah and I looked at each other. I knew what she was thinking. Anybody but Georgie.

Two weeks later the package was addressed to Cecie. "This wool was carded at a mill in Chesterfield," the note said, "but I dyed it for you myself. I hope you like the blue."

Cecie liked the blue. She held the wool up for us all to see. "My girl is doing us proud," she said.

In March Aunt Mattie was favored with fabric for shirting. "For your husband, who was always kind to me," the note read.

I couldn't recollect Uncle Lawrence ever speaking to her. But I said nothing.

The next bundle was for Georgie. "Please give this to my friend," the note said. It was a warm blanket.

At the end of March a plaid came for Aunt Hannah. "I have worked on this a long time," the note said. "I mixed, for this, goldenrod, madder, and peach leaves. I like it much."

Aunt Hannah liked it much, too. She had a dress made of it. "I'm sure the next gift will be for you, Ebie," she said.

I knew there would be nothing for me. And I was right. Do you give a gift to someone who has cut your heart out? Chopped off your fingers?

But by the end of March I didn't care if Walking Breeze sent Aunt Hannah a plaid with all the colors of the rainbow in it. For by then we received word, from the captain of a ship that had just arrived from London, that my father and Uncle Richard were coming home. The house was in an uproar. And then, on the third of April, the *Amity*, Uncle Richard's brig, was sighted running in a fog off Cape Ann.

On the morning of the fourth, as we were preparing to go to the wharf to meet my father and Uncle Richard, Grandfather set off to Cummington to fetch Walking Breeze home.

When Aunt Hannah chided him, saying his son had been gone a year and he ought to come to the wharf and meet him, he looked at her. "This girl is important to me, Hannah," he said. "She represents the future of my mill."

"And what does Cabot represent?" she asked.

He stood holding his hat in his hand in the hall. His only answer was a sigh as he walked out the door.

The *Amity* was carrying six guns. Aunt Mattie said it was God's own miracle that they made it across the Atlantic.

"The miracle," Uncle Lawrence said, "is that your brother had his brig returned to him."

"We have Mr. Burnaby to thank for that," Aunt Hannah said.

I skipped along beside them, scarcely able to contain my excitement. "Who is this Mr. Burnaby?" I asked.

But they got closemouthed then and would not tell me. Let them, I decided. No one could dampen my spirits. No, not even Grandfather, who refused to come and meet him. My father was coming home.

I was the first one to spot him in the crowd of people. "*There* he is!" I screamed.

"Where, where?" Aunt Hannah was frantic.

"Father!" I ran across the wharf, through all the people, the noise and confusion.

"Ebie! My Ebie!" Father was holding Uncle Richard up on one side. A nigra man was holding him on the other. Father released him to embrace me. "Oh, my Ebie, you have grown so! You're a grown young lady!"

"Father!" I held him close. He smelled of tobacco and strong soap, the sea and yes, a bit of liquor thrown in. Oh, it was so good to hold him. Oh, I might never let go.

"Say hello to your uncle Richard, Ebie." He straightened up and I faced the man who was smiling at me.

His hair was still plentiful, but it was streaked with white. His face was pale, his eyes sunken. There were lines around his mouth that I'd never seen before. But he was smiling.

"Oh, Uncle Richard!"

"I lived for your letters, Ebie." He hugged me. Then he looked over my shoulder and I saw a burning light in those sunken eyes. I stepped aside. Because Aunt Hannah was running toward us. And I didn't want to be in the way when she threw herself into his arms.

Chapter Twenty-three

April 6, 1812

Two days later Aunt Hannah had a homecoming party for my father and Uncle Richard in his elegant house in the eastern end of town. Aunt Hannah called it "Republican territory," being that it was settled by the new rich and the old-line Federalists lived in the western end of town.

Aunt Hannah had decorated the house for him and my father occupied a room in it when he was home from sea. I loved visiting my father there. It was a Federal-style house, three stories and each room as neat and polished as Uncle Richard's ships.

So two days after they came home I found myself standing at the kitchen door of Uncle Richard's house with the makings of Marlborough pie in my basket.

I could not get through the door. Walking Breeze stood barring my way.

"You cannot spread your blanket in here."

She was wearing a new plaid frock. Never had

I seen such plaid in Salem. I would have killed for it.

It was the first I'd come face-to-face with her since she arrived home. Yesterday she had spent with Grandfather at his new mill in Waltham. Grandfather paid her more mind these days than he'd paid me all my life. And I was jealous.

Things had come to a curious turn between them. He still would not acknowledge her claim as granddaughter. She no longer wanted him to. But when they'd come home from the mill yesterday, I'd heard her telling him all about how the Shawnees had used bloodroot to paint their faces, and made green paint, from the slimy surface of stagnant water to stain their bodies.

He'd been listening in rapt attention.

"We do not need you here. Go chirp elsewhere, little bird," she said to me now.

"For all your fancy learning, you still talk like an Indian." I knew it was cruel. But she needed taking down.

"Go away." In her hand was a skillet of melted butter.

I saw Cecie stirring a pot over the hearth. I saw the makings of corn pudding, smelled the roast ducklings. Then I spotted the pie shells and the bowl of sliced apples. "You're making Marlborough pie, Cecie," I said. "You know that's mine to make for Uncle Richard!"

"I know nothing of the kind. Except that we

haven't time for your childish tantrums. Go away."

The cheek! I must tell Aunt Hannah how Cecie was getting above herself. "I'm here to make a pie for Uncle Richard!"

"Lower your voice," Cecie said. "Your uncle Richard is sleeping."

"He is in need of quiet," Walking Breeze said. "I just brought him some broth and found him sleeping."

My blood boiled. "Who do you think you *are*, telling me what my uncle Richard needs? I know him better than either of you. And if there's broth to be brought, I'll do the bringing!"

"He doesn't need a chirping little bird like you around," Walking Breeze said.

I could abide no more. I pushed her good. I hit her with my basket. It tilted her skillet of butter onto her white apron and plaid frock. She screamed and set the skillet down. I saw the amber lights in her brown eyes go from smoldering to blazing. "You have insulted me. But I will prevent you from doing the like again!" She grabbed my shoulders and shook me like a child.

I dropped my basket. The sack of flour spilled.

"Leave this place!" Her voice came in panting gasps as we rolled on the floor. "You defile it with your presence!"

I pulled on one of her plaits of hair. I was smaller but strong, too. Soon we were both rolling in the spilled butter and flour, with Cecie trying to separate us.

I struggled. She was strong. I scratched and kicked and slapped her. She hit me in the face.

"What goes on here?"

At the sound of Uncle Richard's voice we both stopped. I scrambled to my feet. "I'm sorry if the noise woke you, Uncle Richard."

His hair was tousled. He was wearing some kind of silken robe over nankeen trousers. "Woke me? I thought I was being attacked by Malays!"

"She's no Malay. She's Shawnee. And trouble."

Uncle Richard looked at Walking Breeze. "You're the girl Hannah told me about."

She stood up, tall and proud. She seemed taller than before she'd gone away. And more of a woman, if that was possible. She carried herself with some newfound pride, all filled up with herself. She swung her plaits around her back and flashed him a smile filled with brilliant white teeth. "Forgive me for behaving like a wildcat, Uncle Richard. I can call you uncle?"

He smiled. "Yes."

"I was much provoked. It was *mat-ou-oui-sah* of me. Bad."

His smile became broader. I could see he was taken with her. I felt everything inside me drop.

"He's not your uncle Richard! He's mine!" I gave her one more push for good measure.

"Ebie, stop that now!" His voice barked, like it did when he was on deck, giving orders.

I stopped.

He was scowling. "Come into the parlor, Ebie,"

he said quietly. Then he turned to Cecie. "Do you think I might have some tea? I brought some bohea."

"Certainly," Cecie said. "My Nancy will bring it, with some fresh cornbread. Go along, now."

We sat on a settle in front of some large windows. A tall case clock ticked quietly in a corner. Carpets from Persia covered the polished floors. Yellow silken damask fell in graceful folds at the windows. In a gleaming cabinet was a set of Canton china. The whole place had about it the air of restrained elegance.

"What in God's name were you about in there, Ebie?"

"She wouldn't let me in the kitchen to make you a Marlborough pie."

"That was about more than a pie. What's going on between you and that girl?"

"Nothing, sir."

"Come, Ebie. Even in my moments of delirium, it came through in your letters."

I looked into his dear face. Oh, it was so good to have him home! I didn't care if he scolded.

"Ebie, you wrote of how you got rid of the quilt. Why did you do her this disfavor?"

"I explained the why of it, Uncle Richard."

Walking Breeze came in with a silver tray then, on which was our repast. She set it down on a marble-topped table. "*Oui-she-e-shi-que-chi*," she said. "Your face is filled with strength. But I would sprinkle something in your tea." She withdrew a small sack from under her apron. "*Chobeka*. Good medicine. Will make you strong, fast."

"Thank you, Walking Breeze."

"You're not going to drink that, are you?" I asked when she left the room.

"I am. From my trips to Sumatra, I learned that some of these tribal people have better ways than we to cure ills. And I need to be strong, fast." He sipped the tea. "Ebie, I have news for you. Your aunt Hannah and I plan to marry in September."

I let out a squeal of delight and jumped up and down on the settle. "Oh, Uncle Richard! Oh, *why?*"

"Why?" He laughed. "I thought you would be happy."

"Oh, I'm *thrilled*. I've prayed for this. But *what made you two decide? After all these years?*"

He smiled sadly and leaned back, crossed his legs, and studied the contents of his tea cup as if the mysteries of the Far East were to be found in it. I thought I saw a film of tears in his eyes. "Prison, Ebie," he said. "Oh, it isn't as if I weren't captured before. But this time was different. It was a British prison. I'm older. I thought about my life and what I had to come home to . . . well, does it matter? We marry in September, so I must be well. And for another reason." He grew grim. I waited.

— 189 —

"I've applied for a commission for privateering. I'm having the *Black Prince* outfitted to cruise and take prizes."

"But you said she wasn't seaworthy!"

"She soon will be. Your father's gone down to the wharves to employ men to get started on her immediately."

This was the way it should be. Us talking about things we both understood. With no Walking Breeze interfering.

"The *Prince* was your grandfather's best privateer in the Revolution," he reminded me. "Until she was burned by the British."

"And then he gave her to you! And you restored her. And made your secret voyage to Sumatra and brought back the first shipment of pepper to America!"

"Seems like a lifetime ago," he said ruefully.

"And you even got her back when she was taken by Malays and *they* put you in prison. Because of the *Prince* you were able to start your own merchant house! Oh, Uncle Richard, I'm so *happy*!" Then I grew sensible of something. "Are you going to war, Uncle Richard?"

"Privateers are the order of the day, Ebie. Our navy is weak. The only way we can win is by capturing their ships and taking them as prizes."

"Oh, I wish I were a boy! I'd go with you. Would you sign me on?"

"No. You have no discipline. You can't take orders."

"I could."

"I don't tolerate fighting on my ships."

Oh, he was clever. "This isn't a ship."

"It's my house."

"Uncle Richard, I told you, she provoked it."

"You have done this girl a grave injustice, Ebie, and I cannot condone it."

"Uncle Richard, what are you saying?"

"That because of you she will be a mill worker. That's a form of slavery. I've seen the mills in England. Does she deserve this?"

"But I did it for everyone in the family! So we wouldn't be badgered with another Georgie. Walking Breeze is nothing but trouble. You don't know the trouble she's given Aunt Hannah already. And the heartache. Do you think Aunt Hannah needs more heartache?"

"If this girl is her sister's daughter, your aunt Hannah will gladly take the good with the bad," he said. "It wasn't your place to do what you did. And I ask you to undo it."

I gaped at him. "Sir?"

"Undo it. Make it right. Surely you can retrieve the quilt and give it back to her."

My head was spinning. "I can't do that, Uncle Richard."

"Is it gone? Was it destroyed?"

"No. Likely it's still at Georgie's."

"Then you can do it. Now, Ebie, we've been friends since you were a child. You have much of your father in you, and he's a good man. But you have disappointed me. To say nothing of how your father would feel if he knew of it."

"Will you tell him?" My heart was hammering.

"I will tell no one. For now."

"For now?" I could scarce speak.

"Yes. I will give you time to do what you must do. I realize it will take a certain amount of time."

Broken days, was all I could think of. He is giving me *broken days*. "How much time?" I whispered.

"I don't know." He stood up. "I'm a patient man, Ebie. I had to learn that in prison. But I learned other things, too. That there is so much trouble in this world, we need to do everything we can, every day of our lives, to stop trouble from happening. Not cause it."

I wanted to cry of a sudden.

He brushed some flour from my face. "I'll give you enough time." His touch was gentle. I knew he loved me. And I knew he was right. Coming from him it *sounded* right. But oh, I couldn't bear it.

"Enough time?" I asked.

"I would rather you did it on your own. The choice is yours. Whether you want to go on being my friend or not."

His *friend*! He was putting our friendship at stake, then. I felt trapped. Something seemed to be pressing against my chest. "You mean if I don't do it we can't be friends anymore?"

He didn't say that. But what he said was worse.

"I shall think less of you, Ebie," he said. That was all. It was enough.

I looked up at him beseechingly.

"I know you won't disappoint me, Ebie," he said. "Now I must go upstairs and try to rest. I'm very tired."

He left me sitting there with tears coming down my cheeks and flour all over my dress. I watched him go into the hall and up the sweeping staircase, thinking I would do anything for Uncle Richard. Always I had felt that way about him.

But how could I do this?

Chapter Twenty-four

April 1812

In the next two weeks war fever came to Salem. The names of Henry Clay, Langdon Cheeves, and John Calhoun were on everybody's lips. A new word was being bandied about. War Hawks.

In my school the girls started collecting the circulars that were left on doorsteps. It became a game to collect them.

Mrs. Peabody said the *Salem Gazette* was offering a prize to the girl who wrote the best essay about the most interesting circular. Mary and I scrambled to find a good one for her to write about.

There were circulars from the Republicans, who wanted war, and from the Federalists, who were against it. Mary even had one that her brother Josiah had printed.

"For the merchants of both parties!" She showed it to me. "The merchants are becoming displeased and violent. After all, they have ships at sea!"

"Will you write about that one?" I asked.

"No, all the merchants care about is money. Let's keep looking."

One fine April morning I found one that nobody had brought to school yet. "It's put out by the Quakers," I told Mary.

She was truly taken with it. "The Quakers have a view that everyone should pay mind to," she said.

Of course, she won the prize. It was a trip to the *Salem Gazette* office. Not only that, they would publish her essay.

Mary was overjoyed. And her brother Josiah, who was to escort her to the newspaper, admitted that the Quakers had put out the finest poster against the war.

Between us we collected two hundred circulars. We each decorated our bedrooms with them.

Aunt Hannah didn't like it. "War is not a game, Ebie," she said, scowling at my bedroom walls. "I recollect the last war. So does everyone in the house. It causes chaos. I hope you never know, firsthand, anyone who dies in one."

Her words cast a pall over me. I did not know why.

The nineteenth of April dawned blue and sunny. I was excused from school, because my father was taking me out for the day. We were going to Fort Lee at Salem Neck to dine with his friend from Harvard College, Captain Rainy.

I dressed with care. As I was tying a ribbon in my hair, I heard Grandfather's voice below stairs.

"Some way to celebrate the Battle of Lexington!"

Who was he bellowing at? I crept down the stairway to see Uncle Lawrence standing in the dining room, hat in hand.

"Denying the President of the United States the services of the militia of Massachusetts!" Grandfather boomed. "Where would our country be, if thirty-seven years ago our militia refused to fight?"

"The president's call for militia is unconstitutional," Uncle Lawrence said quietly. "We are not being invaded."

I thought Grandfather would have apoplexy right there. "British ships were sighted in our waters just yesterday! You call yourself a Patriot?"

"I call myself a thinking American," Uncle Lawrence said.

"Nonsense!" Grandfather was standing at his place at the table. He threw his napkin down.

"Father!" Aunt Hannah said. "Don't excite yourself so. Lawrence, come, sit. Have breakfast."

"I think not," Uncle Lawrence said.

So, Uncle Lawrence had refused his militia to the president! All I could think of was how he'd told Aunt Mattie once that he hadn't been able to make up his mind to have his militia invade Canada, with that Indian girl in our midst, looking at him with her big brown eyes.

Oh, everyone outside this house would say the decision was Governor Strong's. But we knew the governor depended on Uncle Lawrence for that advice.

I always knew that Walking Breeze beset Uncle Lawrence. Had her coming to us affected him that much?

At that moment my father came through the front door. Grandfather saw him and grunted. "It wasn't bad enough," he said to Uncle Lawrence, "that your brother went to beg that king's man in Parliament for favors. Now you refuse the president the best militia in the country!"

"Come in, Cabot," Aunt Hannah said. "Don't pay them mind. They're discussing the war."

"Who isn't?" my father said standing in the hallway. But I could see he sensed it was more than a discussion. "I've come for Ebie," he said.

Grandfather was seated again, sipping his coffee. "I've got one traitor in the family," he said. "And another who cozies up to the king."

"I can't stay, Hannah," Uncle Lawrence said. "I've much to do." Then he said to Grandfather, "Goodday, Father, I'm sorry you think me a traitor. I hope you come to your senses and we can discuss this amiably."

Grandfather waved him out of the room with his fork.

Uncle Lawrence came through the hall and nodded at my father, who gripped his arm. I saw a look of understanding flash between them before Uncle Lawrence went out the door.

"Father, for shame," Aunt Hannah said, "you know Lawrence isn't a traitor. A truer man never lived. As for Cabot, we are much indebted to Mr. Burnaby for securing Richard's release."

"Don't bother, Hannah," Father said. "Are you ready, Ebie?"

"She hasn't had breakfast," Aunt Hannah told him.

"I'll get her tea and biscuits," Father promised. "Get your cloak, Ebie."

I stood in the hall putting it on. "Who is Mr. Burnaby?" I asked. "Why is it that whenever the man's name comes up you all go silent?"

"Good question!" Grandfather boomed. "Cabot, you mean you haven't told your daughter who Burnaby is?"

My father's face went red with anger. "In heaven's name," he blurted out, "keep a still tongue in your head."

His anger shocked us all. Even himself. I thought he would burst with the force of it as we went out the door.

He told me after he stopped to get me biscuits and tea. He told me the way a man tells such a story, terse and plain. In a voice filled with quiet resolve, he spoke the words, looking straight ahead as he held the horse's reins.

"Mr. Burnaby is my real father, Ebie. It's time you knew."

I stared at him, struck dumb.

"During the war, Burnaby was a captain in the British navy. He came ashore in Salem with his men, to my mother's house. They forced their way in. She fed them. Then she had them arrested. But Burnaby was very taken with her. He came back. They became friends. Her marriage to your grandfather had not been happy for a long time. That's why I was born."

Certainly he'd taken leave of his senses.

"It's true, Ebie, all of it. I always meant to tell you. But I wanted you to be old enough to understand."

Oddly, I did understand. Once I got past the shock of it, it clarified a lot for me. "It's why Grandfather treats you so shabbily," I said.

"Yes."

"Oh, Father, I'm so glad!"

"Glad?"

"Now I don't feel so bad that he doesn't love us. But why do you abide such treatment from him? You don't have to."

He put an arm around me. "He's a bitter old man, Ebie. If I gave him his due now, it would kill him. I'm beyond his taunts and hurts."

We drove in silence to the wharf, wrapped in our own thoughts. Then I became sensible of something. "He isn't my grandfather then, is he?"

"For all intents and purposes he is, Ebie. And I would have you continue to respect him."

But he wasn't my grandfather! *He was Walking Breeze's grandfather. Not mine.*

That truth struck me in the face, like cold water. I wanted to laugh. Walking Breeze was his grandchild! Not me! I stole a look at my father's profile. He was solemn, thinking. I would know more, I determined. But he's told me enough for now. I minded how difficult the telling must have been for him.

In spite of my father's revelation and the confusion it caused in me, we had a wonderful day together. Just being with him, having him all to myself, was enough to make it a good day.

Captain Rainy met our barge at the fort. We had an elegant noon meal. At the table were other officers and their wives. They asked my father about his recent trip, about Dartmoor Prison, about feeling for us in England.

Listening to my father answer their questions, I realized that he was a brilliant man. Others recognized and respected his opinions. Yet he was so modest! And so handsome! Oh, not as tall as Uncle Lawrence. And he was somewhat balding. But he seemed to have a new sense of purpose. And it added to his presence.

On the way home in the chaise he told me that Captain Rainy was relinquishing command of the fort, in favor of someone who could take charge of its coastal defenses. "Your uncle Lawrence is taking over," he said. "He's a good man, Ebie. Don't listen to that folderol your grandfather says about him being a traitor. He put a lot of thought into his decision about the militia. Your uncle Lawrence is a very moral man. He knows, in his heart, what is right. And he'll do it, no matter what people say of him."

I nodded. "But how do we know when we're doing the right thing, Father?"

He drew up the horse's reins in front of our house. "We don't always, Ebie. Answers don't come easily. At least they never have, to me. I've done many a wrong thing in my time. But I've always tried to make up for it."

"And have you?"

"Not always," he said sadly.

More secrets. I wondered if it had to do with my mother. He never spoke of her. No one did. Did he ever think of her? Something was burdening him.

"Will you tell me more about your real father?"

"Someday, yes."

"Is he a good person? Or cruel, like those king's men who imprisoned Uncle Richard?"

"He's a good man, Ebie. Go in now, it's late."

I went in. But not before I hugged him. I supposed that I would never truly understand my father. But I know I loved him more that day, than I had ever before.

Chapter Twenty-five

May 2, 1812

Dear Ebie:

I write to beg your forgiveness for not having returned your favor before this. But I have a new address these days and your letter just caught up with me.

Ebie, I can scarce believe the good fortune of my words, even as I pen them to you. I have lately become a member of this country's fledgling navy. I just signed on with the crew of the Constitution here in Boston.

The roster was not yet filled. And Captain Isaac Hull, under whom I will serve, went to sea when he was only fourteen, so he did not consider my age as something to render me unfit.

The ship is so beautiful, Ebie! Her frame is made of Georgia oak, her masts from white pine from Maine, and white oak from our state makes up her deck. Paul Revere made her bell and the copper for her bottom. The billowing of her sails in the wind is celestial, nothing less.

No, I am not in the complement of thirty or

so boys who sleep in canvas hammocks on the berth deck. I am an officer, though of the junior kind.

My uncle's name — Crowninshield — does count for something. And he wrote a fine letter to recommend me. I know I can work and do him proud.

Yes, I miss you. And the fine times we had in Salem, though they seem like a hundred years ago now. And I tender my congratulations that you won our bet and will honor it in the true spirit in which it was made.

I have the perfect gift for you. No, it is not Mary Wollstonecraft's book. And no, I cannot tell you what it is, for it is to be a surprise.

Part of it is a visit. I don't know when. We are to clear the harbor here soon. But when we put into port again, I shall come and see you. And I will bring the present, as it can only be delivered in person.

Now you must hate me for keeping you on tenterhooks. Well, you shall have to stew in the juices of your own impatience. Be assured, the wait will be well worth it.

Until we meet then, dear girl, please be assured that you have it in your power to gratify me with your forgiveness for my tardy reply to your delightful letter.

I remain ever your dear friend and faithful
servant, Benjamin.

Chapter Twenty-six

June 1812

War came in mid-June. And everyone in Salem acted like six kinds of a fool. They celebrated or they gathered in knots on street corners in ugly moods, depending on their politics.

Mrs. Peabody near had a case of hysteria. "Girls, girls," she assembled us that day, wringing her hands. "Mr. Madison has started his war. Go right home. Don't linger, for the danger."

The way she spoke, you would think British warships were in Marblehead Bay. The night of the twenty-second, when the war news reached us, some people overthrew vendors' carts and broke windows. Some went to church. Others blew conch shells and burned bonfires far into the night. The excitement in the air was better than the day before Thanksgiving. It lifted me out of blue devils I'd been in for two months.

It made me forget how much I had come to hate Walking Breeze.

But only for the moment. And then I put my mind to hating her again with all my powers. Because she was growing steadily in everyone's esteem. While I was being pushed into the background.

"You've always been in the background," Mary said. "It's just that now someone's stepped in front of you."

I supposed she was right. But it hurt just the same that all Grandfather talked about at supper was the wonderful job Walking Breeze was doing supervising the dyeing at the mill. You would think that getting a deeper red color would solve the problems of the world. Maybe move the British warships that were bottling up our whole coast.

Walking Breeze still lived with us. Which meant that sometimes she helped serve at the table. I never could figure out how she managed to look so full of vinegar after working at the mill all day. The only telltale sign of her work was the blue or red dye stains on her long brown fingers.

Aunt Hannah had nothing but words of praise for her, too. Because the concoction Walking Breeze had given Uncle Richard had worked. He was just about his old self again. Then, too, Aunt Hannah had to share some pride in Walking Breeze. After all, her friend Sarah Bryant had prepared her well.

As for my father, I scarcely saw him. He and Uncle Richard were busy with the *Prince*. Uncle Lawrence spent his days at Fort Lee. Aunt Mattie and Aunt Hannah were helping resettle the families of the children who had worked in the mill.

I was alone. My grandfather wasn't my grandfather. I had no love for the man, but every day this fact cut into me like a knife. I felt anchorless, cut from my moorings and adrift.

And then, to add to everything, my father announced that he was going to war.

The last day of June commissions came through for all the privateers that were waiting in Salem Harbor. Uncle Richard was to sail on July third. And my father announced that he was going with him. Of course, Aunt Hannah had to have a party on the *Prince*. She said it was to celebrate the ship's restoration. But I think it was to celebrate her coming marriage. I know this: The *Prince* had no use for the gifts people brought.

It was at that party, right on the quarterdeck, that my father stood, glass in hand, and said he was sailing with Uncle Richard. He looked right at my grandfather, too, when he said it. Like he was spiting him, going. Because the old man had captained the *Prince* as a privateer in the Revolution.

I couldn't wait until everyone finished congratulating Father. For what? Because he was making a brassbound fool of himself by going off to get killed? He'd just gotten *back*. I had tears in my eyes. Mary had to restrain me. Then, when he was standing alone with Uncle Richard, she let me go. I ran to him.

"I don't want you to go." I sobbed into his frock coat.

He patted my shoulder. "Come, Ebie, would you deny me this adventure? Should Uncle Richard have all the sport?"

Next thing I knew, Uncle Richard was leading me away, his large hand in mine. "Come below deck, Ebie, and see my cabin."

I knew he wanted to talk and I didn't want to. I didn't need to hear about Walking Breeze now. But there was nothing for it. I had to go with him.

"I'll have your father back in three weeks, Ebie. And he's an excellent seaman. But you know that. So what's plaguing you?"

"My father told me who his father is," I said.

He thought for a moment. From above us came the sounds of music from his crew. Sea chanties. And the thump of people dancing.

"I'm not his granddaughter." I blurted it out, tearfully.

He nodded and sighed. "That shouldn't make you feel of the inferior sort."

"Well, it does. Walking Breeze is his granddaughter. You tell me, Uncle Richard, how can I do right by her now?"

He took a sip from his glass. "Do it for your father," he said.

"My father?"

"Yes. You see, something's weighing on him, Ebie. He needs to make peace with his sister, Thankful."

"She's dead."

"Making peace with her daughter would serve him as well."

"Why does he need to make peace with Thankful?"

"It was she who told him your grandfather wasn't *his* father. She wrote to him of it while she was out west. When he received the letter he ran away. Your aunt Hannah and I had to bring him back. He's never forgiven Thankful for that."

So that was what father had meant when he'd said there was something he hadn't made up for in his life.

"He doesn't know that Walking Breeze is her daughter," I said stubbornly.

"He feels it. Same as your uncle Lawrence does. But it would help if it were made clear for him. Your father *needs* to do this. But only you can help him."

"I can't do it, Uncle Richard," I said.

"You can. You have it in you to do it. You're a good person."

"I'm not. I don't *want* to be a good person." I started to cry.

He held me close then. And what he said surprised me. "What makes you think any of us want to be good people, Ebie? You know, I never agreed with these Puritan preachers, who tell us we're all inherently bad. I think we're all inherently good. And we fight against it, all our lives."

They fired the *Prince*'s guns in salute when they cleared Salem Harbor. Everyone on the wharf cheered. I stood and waved. But I was crying, not cheering. I never felt less like cheering in my life.

Things quieted down. The militia marched on the Fourth of July and nobody threw rocks at them, which, in Salem, was taken as a sign that people were turning in favor of the war.

The privateers were bringing in so many prizes to the port of Salem that the people couldn't help feeling pride. Governor Strong came to our church. But Grandfather wouldn't go. He went to New Meeting in Marblehead, where Reverend Bartlet preached for the war and against the impurity of women.

Aunt Hannah said both views seemed to please the old man immensely.

Aunt Hannah was taken up with wedding plans. Mary and I were to be bridesmaids, along with Aunt Mattie and Martha Crowninshield. Aunt Hannah had gone to school with Martha, who by virtue of marriage was aunt to my friend Benjamin.

And now another war waged in our house. Between Grandfather and Aunt Hannah. He wanted the wedding in his house in what would be a fashionable display of the new wedding customs being practiced by the wealthy.

Aunt Hannah said no. It would be on the quarterdeck of the *Prince*, "Where it should have been twenty years ago."

"Unheard of!" Grandfather yelled. "It's heathen!"

Aunt Hannah said it wasn't heathen. And that Parson Bentley had agreed to it. She didn't tell Grandfather that she and Uncle Richard had given a substantial donation to the parson for a new roof on the church.

The parson told me that himself one day when he came to tea. "Tell you the truth, Ebie," he said, "I'd have married them on the *Prince* anyway. I think it's a grand idea."

He would.

Aunt Hannah enlisted me as support against Grandfather. I was glad for the role. I didn't care if they got married on Griffin's Wharf, as long as they wed. To me that wasn't the point. What was the point was that I was going against Grandfather. And that was enough.

On July seventeenth, Mary and I went to the wharves. A ship had arrived from the West Indies and we needed spices for Aunt Hannah's wedding cake.

When we got home, Aunt Hannah was waiting in the parlor. She had a letter in her hand, and the look on her face was the same as it had been the day she'd called us down from the garret to say she had a letter from Uncle Louis.

"Your friend, Benjamin, is coming to call on you," she said.

Mary and I jumped up and down in delight.

"He is bringing your present."

Her face was very white. *Dear God,* I thought, *Benjamin has taken leave of his senses. He's bringing me a monkey brought into Boston from the West Indies, I suppose. Or some other ludicrous gift.*

"It is a friend," Aunt Hannah said with great effort. Then she held her arms out to me. "Oh, Ebie, he's bringing my sister Abby's boy. They are serving together on the *Constitution*."

Tears were streaming down her face.

Chapter Twenty-seven

Mid-July 1812

"I am going to be requiring southern cotton in my mill," Grandfather said to Jemmy across the supper table.

Aunt Hannah's fork paused in midair. I knew what she was thinking, that Grandfather hadn't spoken to Aunt Abby in years. And now he was going to be needing southern cotton from their plantation.

"We shall be glad to provide it, suh," Jemmy said. "Our Sea Isle cotton crop is better than upland cotton. We fertilize it with salt-marsh mud."

His real name was Jeremiah Videau. When he came up the walk with Benjamin that afternoon, the first thing I'd looked for was the laughing blue eyes of the little boy I'd played with on my visit to South Carolina with Aunt Hannah.

The little boy was gone. But the laughing blue eyes were there.

The second thing I'd looked for was any sign of dementia. Grandfather always said that southerners were slovenly, power starved, and half mad. I saw only sanity in Jemmy's face.

I also saw substance, an elegant manner, blond hair, and something else. I could not name it at first. And then I could.

Caring. When he spoke to you, Jemmy truly cared. And I heard the southern drawl. It captivated me right off.

Benjamin had presented him proudly. "I told you I'd bring you a present, didn't I, Ebie?"

I was awfully glad for that sea serpent. And for Benjamin! His face was set in the determined lines of a man now. I hugged him. We had a pleasant hour in Aunt Hannah's garden, the four of us. Then Benjamin had to go to his uncle's house. As Jemmy walked him to the front gate, Mary whispered savagely to me. "He's your cousin. Stop looking so smitten!"

"Mary, I'm not smitten."

"Then what are you?"

"Right now, I think I'm a three-masted square rigger, drifting rudderless and with limp sails on a becalmed ocean, off course and taken for lost by those at home," I said, "and Jemmy is a southwesterly trade wind."

Walking Breeze came into the dining room that night bearing a platter of steamed vegetables as if it were a sacrifice to the gods. In the flickering candlelight, she looked like some primitive goddess herself, all bronze and tall and graceful in her blue and white dress with the spotless apron.

Jemmy's blue eyes were startled into fascination. Everyone who saw her for the first time looked that way.

"Our girl here is wearing a dress she wove and dyed herself," Grandfather said.

"Blue," Jemmy said. "Sorry, suh, but ah can't promise you any indigo. It was my people's money crop until the Revolution, when England turned to the East Indies for it. Then, we had a destructive caterpillar in the indigo fields, too."

"What is your money crop now?" Grandfather asked.

"Cotton, sweet potatoes, and corn." He was still looking at Walking Breeze.

"How are your dear parents?" Aunt Hannah asked.

"Well, ma'am. And busy, since they purchased Yamassee on St. Helena's Island. And Father is acquirin' another plantation on Ladies' Island." Then to Grandfather, "Ah shall write to my father and convey your needs. And when this war is ovah, ah shall enjoy the personal honor of runnin' cotton up heah for you."

"Come tour our mill tomorrow," Grandfather invited.

"Ah have an invite from Uncle Lawrence to see Fort Lee in the mornin', suh, but ah'd admire to give you my afternoon."

"My, you sound so like your dear father," Aunt Hannah said.

Jemmy blushed. I thought I would swoon. I was entranced with him. Even when he talked about salt-marsh mud.

He stayed with us for a week. In that time, he, Benjamin, Mary, and I had a picnic on Winter Island. We took him to the stone lookout tower. He told us about his brothers Ben, twelve, and Sumner, ten, and about the blue doors in the negroes' low-country houses, painted from old indigo pots, to keep out "hants" or ghosts. We told him about Salem's witches.

Aunt Hannah took him to tea twice at the houses of friends. Both times I sat next to him, while he balanced delicate Canton china cups on his knee with all the practice of a Salem aristocrat, in his smart uniform.

We went to an evening of entertainment at the East India Marine Hall, where the wives of leading merchants dressed in Oriental gowns. Parson Bentley invited us on a fishing party and we ate hot chowder on the boat and Grandfather opened a bottle of Madeira that said *Astrea 1787.*

Grandfather showed him his countinghouse. Later we went to the Sun Tavern for a noon meal, where we sat at a polished table and ate creamed lobster. And Simon Forrester came over and offered Grandfather a share in a cargo of foodstuffs going to the Iberian Peninsula.

"The British will not interfeah with such a voyage?" Jemmy asked.

Forrester was a skinflint merchant, with a temper like a tempest, but I thought him most wonderful when he took Jemmy's hand and welcomed him to Salem. "The British still hope to encourage peace with New Englanders, for our trade," he said.

I prayed the week would never end. But it did. Before Jemmy left, however, something happened that brought me and him together in a way that no creamed lobster or fishing party could.

Georgie turned up missing.

Well, not truly missing. Aunt Hannah knew where she'd been sighted. "At the Quaker meetinghouse," she said. "Mr. Phinney, the fishmonger, saw her there." We stood in the hallway. It was getting on to dusk, Friday.

Jemmy and I had just returned from Crowninshield's Wharf, where there had been a party to see off another privateer. We'd danced ourselves silly, reeling to fiddle music. The July dusk was sweet and thick with sea smells and a kind of magic.

Aunt Hannah wrung her hands. "Georgie never goes out in the day. And what is she doing with the Quakers?"

"She meets at their council fires. They protest the war," Walking Breeze came into the hall. "They are people of peace."

"I know what Quakers are about," Aunt Hannah said. "But why is Georgie with them?"

"I will bring her home for you," was all Walking Breeze would say. And with that, she went out the front door.

Aunt Hannah pressed her hands to her temples. "The Friends. Georgie has been intimate with the *Friends*. Oh, we must get her back before my father finds out she is in the streets."

"We'll fetch her home for you, Aunt Hannah." Jemmy led her to a chair and called for Cecie to bring her some tea. "Come on, Ebie," he said, "Walking Breeze may need help."

The Quaker meetinghouse was a mile past the Common. Walking Breeze was about a block ahead of us, rushing along in great strides, her skirts flapping.

"Is she our cousin?" Jemmy asked me, "as Uncle Lawrence said when ah visited him at the fort?"

I had been expecting the question. "She lays claim to the family as Aunt Thankful's daughter," I said.

"In heaven's name, then why does our grandfather treat her like a servant?"

"She has no proof of who she claims to be."

A scowl came over his handsome face. "Suppose she is kin? It would be hurtful to treat her so."

"Suppose she isn't. Wouldn't it be wrong to treat her as such?"

He shook his head and put a hand under my

elbow as we rushed along. "Where ah come from, we'd take her on her word. A person's word is his honor where ah come from."

Walking Breeze was walking very fast. Jemmy took my hand and we increased our pace.

"And family is of the first consideration," he went on. "Ah know Grandfather disowned my mother. Ah know how grievous hurt that made her. And ah heard how he treats your father. That Indian girl doesn't have a prayer with him."

His hand was cool and firm in mine.

"Ah heard he isn't inordinately fond of you, either."

I shrugged. "Aunt Hannah is good to me."

"He nevah forgave my mother because she ran off with a slaveholder. But he treats those girls in his mill worst than we treat our nigras. Look heah, Ebie, it isn't fittin' that he's got that girl workin' in his mill. I'd look kindly on it if you helped her."

He smiled at me. I felt some well of rushing warmth bubbling inside me. "What could I do?" I asked.

"Ah don't know, but we'll study on it. Come on, let's run. My, that girl is as swift as a hound dog in coon season."

We ran. "All these yeahs ah've heard of my family up heah. Ah remember you somewhat, Ebie. But ah had no idea you turned into such a pretty little thing."

He could ask me to run off and join the crew of the *Constitution* and I would do it just then.

Mary always said I had no backbone. What was the virtue in having backbone, I wondered, as I struggled for my next breath. Aunt Hannah had always been proud of hers. And where had it gotten her? She was marrying Uncle Richard twenty years late.

Outside the meetinghouse, Walking Breeze scowled at us. "Have respect for their council fires," she said.

Her air of superiority nettled me. But Jemmy nodded in assent and, with his hand still in mine, we followed her into the plain room. She slipped into a bench on the women's side, directly behind Georgie. I could not believe it! Georgie had always refused to go to our church. Now she sat meekly in a plain gray cloak and white bonnet, listening.

Jemmy and I stood in back. There was no minister. The people just sat in silence, meditating. A man got up and spoke. "If we condone a war against the Indians, we slaughter innocents," he said. Then he sat down.

Another man stood. "I agree with Friend Shields. And I offer my services to help distribute the bulletins this night."

A few more people said things in kind. Then the meeting was over. I took a handbill being distributed at the door. It said the Indians were innocent pawns in the war.

Outside, Georgie smiled at Walking Breeze. "They speak for our people." Her eyes were bright.

"Come home with me," Walking Breeze suggested.

Georgie saw me and Jemmy then. "Are you listening to this little fool now?" she asked Walking Breeze.

"I come to keep you from danger," Walking Breeze said. "Something serious bad could happen to you in the street. People's faces are full of storm because of the war."

Georgie hugged her handbills close. "Never have I felt more strongly about what I am. And it's about time I stood up for it." Then she handed the circulars to Walking Breeze and took off her Quaker bonnet and cloak.

Underneath she had on her Indian dress. "Now I'll distribute the bulletins," she said.

I gasped. "You can't!"

"I can and I must," she said.

Walking Breeze pulled her around the corner, out of sight before anyone could see her in the Indian clothes. "You ask for trouble," she said. "Please put the cloak on."

"The time has come for me," Georgie insisted again. "Will you accompany me? Will you stand for what you are? Or have they corrupted you?"

For the first time since I'd known her, Walking Breeze did not know what to do.

Jemmy did. Up until now he'd kept a still tongue in his head. Now he spoke. "Ah say theah, Georgie, ah'm proud to make your acquaintance. Ah'm Abby's boy, Jemmy." He stuck out his hand.

Georgie stared at him and for a moment I thought she would physically attack him in that naval uniform. "I didn't know your mother," she said tersely.

"You'd like her, Georgie. She had the same spirit you have, when she lived heah as a girl. You think she eloped out that window because she was a milksop? No. She had fire inside her. Just like you. And she raised me that way, too. One thing she told me, Georgie, that's held me in good stead. You want to know what it is?"

Clearly, Georgie was taken with him. It was the southern accent that did it. She nodded yes.

He leaned toward her. " 'Always pick your fights,' she said. Yessir. It's a rule ah live by. And this fight, it isn't yours tonight, Georgie."

"Yes, it is."

"No, it's theahs." He gestured his blond head to the Quakers. "They have the protection of theah religion. What do you have if you get caught handing these things out in those Indian clothes? The town fathers will clap you in leg irons! And what good will *that* do your people? Now, if you put those Quaker clothes back *on* and let us walk with you for protection, why ah'd say my mother will be right proud of you when ah tell her what you did tonight."

Georgie blinked. She was mesmerized. "She would?"

"She would."

But she wasn't convinced.

"Ah tell you, Georgie, what's important heah is that you deliver the handbills. Not what you wear deliverin' 'em."

She nodded. All the while, Jemmy was leading us in the direction of home. He kept a steady stream of talk coming, too. And we kept off the main streets.

As discreetly as possible, Walking Breeze, Georgie, and I left the circulars on front stoops. Jemmy did not touch them.

Mary told me why later. "He would have been in trouble handing out anti-war circulars and wearing that uniform," she said.

I had never thought of it. Apparently Jemmy had. But it was what he did later that proved what kind of person he really was.

At supper, Grandfather raised his glass just as Walking Breeze came into the room with a platter of fish. "I propose a toast," he said. "To Walking Breeze. For bringing Georgie safely home."

"Heah, heah," Jemmy said. And when I started to speak, he scowled at me. So I kept silent.

We were walking in the garden after supper. It was his last night. Tomorrow he was going back to Boston.

"Why did you do that at supper?" I asked.

"Because Walking Breeze needs all the good credit she can get with the old man, Ebie," he drawled.

Summer bugs were droning. Birds were making

going-to-sleep sounds. From the open windows of the house I could hear our elders at coffee in the parlor.

"It's up to us young people to get it all of a piece again, this family," he said. "They can't. Will you help me?"

I said I would.

"Tell you what. We'll put our heads together. And we'll both study on how to get the old man to accept that girl. You'd like that, wouldn't you, Ebie?"

He didn't say like, he said lak. I told him I lakked it fine.

"Uncle Lawrence thinks she's Aunt Thankful's daughter. And that's good enough for me. Ah admire him. My mother still speaks of how he helped her elope that night." He sighed. "This family is so torn apart, Ebie. Your folks are like a family of bears who've been in hibernation too long. Why, they're the most ornery set of folks ah've ever set eyes on. All except for you. Ah don't know how you managed to bloom into such a sweet little thing in this briar patch of people."

"Do all southern boys speak like this?" I asked.

"Only sayin' what's true. So you'll help me, then? We'll get this fool family back in one piece."

I said yes.

"Ah'll write to you, soon's ah get back to Boston. Would you like that?"

He didn't say write, he said rat. So I said yes again. What else could I do? The way he looked at me, the earnestness of him, made it seem rat. Not right, no. But rat.

Yes, I was smitten with him, Mary was right. Not in a romantic way, but in a way that was far more damaging.

He represented family to me. Something I had wanted to believe in all my life. They believed in family down South.

I decided I would do what must be done about Walking Breeze. It was time. My time of the broken days was finished. Jemmy had told me that in his own way.

We'd had enough broken days in this family.

I would retrieve the quilt from Georgie's. I didn't have to admit I'd put it there. Uncle Richard wouldn't tell.

But I would not act before Jemmy wrote. I wanted him to be part of it. We were in this together. Somehow I would contrive to tell him I'd found the quilt by accident.

When he left, he said they'd be in Boston well into August. His captain was awaiting orders.

But he never wrote.

I waited two weeks. August came. I felt betrayed. He had plenty of time to write, even with all his duties.

"All his flowery words were empty," I told Mary.

"Give him more time," she said.

"I was a fool ever to believe anything he said."

If Mary agreed, she did not say it. Of course she

did not know what hung in the balance. I'd never confided in her about the quilt. She thought I was waiting for Jemmy to suggest how we could get Walking Breeze back into the family.

But I needed nobody to tell me I'd been a fool to believe in Jemmy. Or in family. So I did the only thing I could do. I did nothing.

Chapter Twenty-eight

Mid-August 1812

"I've got the miseries, Ebie," Mary said. "I feel in my bones that something awful is going to befall me."

We were standing on the wharf, in the middle of a crowd of people. The *Prince* was back, with two prizes. One was a British lumber vessel, the other the *Liverpool Packet*, out of Nova Scotia.

I took Mary's hand. It was cold. Yet the day was hot. It was the nineteenth of August.

"Are you ailing?" I asked.

"Not in the normal way. I'm pure sad. It came on me this morning."

I hugged her. Mary's "gift" of second sight was a plague. We often laughed about it. If Mary lived in witch hunt times, she, not Georgie, would be the first brought in for questioning in Salem.

Just then I sighted Uncle Richard and my father, standing on the quarterdeck, talking with customs' men.

Mary said I should go to them. She did not want

to afflict me with her misery. It had nothing to do with me, she said. I believed her.

On the last day of August my father took me to tea at the Widow Berry's. She lived on Chestnut Street and had two sons at Dartmouth. He wanted me to meet her because he was taking rooms at her house now that Uncle Richard and Aunt Hannah were getting married. The Widow Berry was younger than I expected. And prettier. And I think she had designs on my father. Which was all right with me. What my father needed was to have a woman with designs on him.

We were coming home in the chaise when he looked at me. "How would you like to live with Aunt Hannah when she marries?" he asked.

"Aunt Hannah?" I thought for a moment. Yes, I thought, of course. Aunt Hannah will be living in Uncle Richard's house when she marries. "Why can't I live with you?" I asked.

"I'll be away at times. So will Uncle Richard. Aunt Hannah could use your companionship. And you need her influence."

"Do you like the Widow Berry?" I asked.

"She's a fine woman. She has warmth and spirit."

It was the first I'd ever heard him speak so of a woman. His shoulders were hunched forward and he looked straight ahead, as if to guard his thoughts. I felt encouraged and became excited at the thought of moving. A contentment settled over me.

Then we were stopped in the street by a young man brandishing handbills. "The *Constitution*," he was yelling.

My heart lurched. Father took a handbill. It told of how, on August nineteenth, the *Constitution* had successfully engaged in battle with the British ship *Guerriere*. Captain Hull had ordered broadside after broadside fired into the enemy ship, which soon lost her masts.

The *Constitution* had put in at Boston Harbor yesterday. The handbill listed her wounded and dead.

One of the names of the dead was Jeremiah Videau, midshipman.

August nineteenth! That was the day Mary had her miseries.

I burst into tears. My father held me. Dead! Jemmy! I could not believe it! I was inconsolable. My dear sweet Jemmy. No, I could not believe it.

The first thing I did was tear down the war circulars from my walls. They were a bad omen. When Aunt Hannah first saw them she'd said she hoped I'd never know what it was like to lose someone in a war, didn't she? Well, now I knew.

I don't have too much of a clear memory of what happened after that. People came knocking on my door, but I wouldn't let them in.

I heard them talking downstairs at supper. A

houseful. My family fights like dogs with each other until there is trouble. Then they sit down and break bread together.

Footsteps then in the hall. And Uncle Richard's voice. "Ebie, let me in. I've a letter for you. From Benjamin."

It was dark by then. He held the lamp while I read:

" 'Dear Ebie: We left Boston earlier than we expected . . .' "

Oh, the words were a blur of phrases that ran together in my head. " 'Orders came through . . . Jemmy wanted to write to you. He did not have the chance . . . terrible battle . . . Jemmy acquitted himself bravely . . . he spoke of you often . . . so glad I could bring him to you when I did . . . something he wanted to tell you . . .' "

"I wish I'd met him," Uncle Richard said.

I blew my nose. "He knew all the family secrets, Uncle Richard," I said. "He wanted to make the family right again. We were going to do something about Walking Breeze. Together."

"You can still do it. For him."

My head swam with the thought. "What did they do with his body?"

"It was sent home."

Home. To that place of sea grasses and salt-marsh mud, that place where they painted doors blue to keep away hants, where a person's word was taken on honor. And family was the first consideration. "I'll go there someday, Uncle Richard," I said. "I can't go to the service tonight. What's the point? Jemmy won't be there."

"It's for your aunt Hannah," he said huskily. "Parson Bentley knew Jemmy's mother when she was a girl. I'll make your excuses to them."

I heard everyone leave for church after supper. Then I heard the booming of guns from the harbor. Salutes for the victory of the *Constitution*. The guns echoed in my bones.

I went downstairs. Walking Breeze was clearing away the supper table. Rays of setting sun slanted through the windows. I stood watching her languid movements.

She must have sensed I was watching, and turned.

We had not spoken since that last night Jemmy was here, when we brought Georgie home from the Quaker meeting. A terrible moment of silence passed through, on its way to eternity, as we stood looking at each other.

"He was kind to me, your Jemmy," she said.

I nodded. I knew she was giving me something, calling him mine. Was it a peace offering? No, I decided, it was pity.

"We all move toward death every day," she said.

I nodded and proceeded to ask her what I needed to know. "Tell me what happens when the broken days are finished and one does not complete a task."

"We go into the next world without finishing

— 230 —

our work in this one. Our spirit will never rest."

I believed that. It made more sense than anything I'd heard in our church. My spirit was having trouble resting now.

"Do you want to be known as a granddaughter?" I asked.

She shrugged. "I could not complete my task of delivering the quilt to Aunt Hannah. I do not deserve to be known as granddaughter."

Well, that was so much nonsense. And I think she knew it, but her pride was getting in the way.

"But if I retrieved the quilt and gave it to them. Would you want that?" I pushed.

Her brown eyes went wide. "You would do this thing?"

"I'm thinking on it. But I need to know if it's what you want, Walking Breeze," I told her. "You told me once that you didn't want him as a grandfather. Because he's a wicked man."

She sighed and ran her fingers lightly over a cut glass bowl on the table. "It would make my spirit small to beg for his love," she said.

"I don't think you'd have to beg for it," I said. "Not if he knew who you were. Besides, you two get on so well."

"We Shawnee children are taught that our elders are due great respect."

"Walking Breeze, it's more than that. You're a proud person. Yet you've taken so much from us in this house. Why?"

She smiled. "You would not understand."

"Try me."

"For my mother. These are her people. I honor her memory."

For her mother. So that was it. I thought of my own mother. Could I do as much for her? "Still, you and Grandfather have found a common ground. Why, if he accepted you as granddaughter, you could run the mill for him. You're that smart."

She said nothing. Honor at work again, likely. Or pride. That was it. And I must allow her to keep her pride. I must let her think she was doing me the favor here. I owed her that much, for what I'd put her through, didn't I?

"Walking Breeze, my time of broken days to get the quilt is running out. Do you want my spirit never to rest?"

She met my eyes. Then she did something I never thought she would do for me. She smiled.

A church bell tolled somewhere as I came into Georgie's yard. The evening light was sweet and distilled. I knocked on the front door.

"She's around back." Nathaniel Hathorne pointed toward Georgie, who was bent over a cage in the yard.

She looked dirtier than I'd ever seen her. She put an arm up as if to shield herself. "What do you want?"

I felt dismay. She'd been behaving with the Quakers.

"How are you keeping?"

"How does a prisoner keep?"

"Who's made you a prisoner?"

She grunted. "The family. Grandfather. Someone told him I was seen in Indian clothes."

"But you only had your cloak off for a *minute* or two."

She shrugged. "This is Salem," she said. "So now I'm not ever allowed to go out of my house. He had a man come to see me. The man said they would put me away for a crazy. They would, too. So I can't go out."

Dear God! I did not know what to say. So I spoke of other things. "Where did you get the bird?" It was a red bird, and it was hurt. She smoothed its feathers and spoke softly to it.

"The Prophet found it the other day. A bone in its shoulder is broken."

"Are you going to keep it and make it well?"

"No, I'm going to let it go."

"It can't fly. It will die."

"No more birds in cages. I let them all go. See?" And she gestured to the fence where her cages sat, all empty. "All except Octavius."

"Why did you let them go?"

"You have to ask that?"

I sighed. "I suppose the family is trying to protect you, Georgie," I said. "They don't want the town fathers to put you away." I knew my words were lies, but I said them anyway. "When you love someone you try to protect them."

"Then this love is a cage."

"I suppose it could be."

"Then I must let this little one go. And take his chances."

I prayed for the right words. "Why not keep his cage door open? Then he could fly when he feels strong enough."

She stood up. So did I. It was as if a great matter had been settled between us. "You've come for the quilt," she said.

I drew in my breath. "How did you know?"

"I recollect the quilt Hannah worked on when I was a child. And I know you and Walking Breeze are at each other's throats."

"Why didn't you tell her the quilt was here?"

She smiled. "Because, when you brought it here, I knew it for what it was. Don't you know what it is?"

What game were we playing now? "No."

"It's a cage," she said. "And that's why I won't give it back to you."

No amount of arguing would change her mind. We went into the house. "Walking Breeze has come into her own without their name," she said. "She doesn't need it."

She took my measure carefully. "Once they know she is family, they will try to make her like them. Like they tried with me. And you."

"What's wrong with me?" I said indignantly.

She walked around the house, touching things.

"You took the quilt from her, didn't you?"

I had no answer for that.

"The way she is now, her cage door is open. If they know she is a granddaughter, they will close it against the world. And she will become like me."

"It doesn't have to be that way, Georgie." I wanted to tell her that Walking Breeze was strong. That she'd been raised Shawnee. But that would imply *she* was weak. And insult her.

"No, but it is that way. And that's what makes it so sad."

There was no profit in arguing. Her mind was set. I decided to leave. Then I had a thought.

It was more by way of a revelation. "Who do you hate more?" I asked. "Your father? Or our family?"

"My hate for my father keeps me alive."

"Then mayhap your cage is not made of love," I said, "but of hate. Did you ever think that your hate is making you a prisoner?"

I saw what my words did to her. They sat on her, like vultures perched on her shoulders.

"And that's what will happen to Walking Breeze. She'll start to hate, too. She could hate me, yes. But she could hate you, if she finds out you kept me from returning the quilt."

"How could she find this out?" Her eyes narrowed. I had her thinking.

"I could tell her."

She threw a wooden bowl at me then. I dodged it and escaped out the door.

"Look alive," Octavius was yelling. "Spaniards on deck!"

I ran all the way home, sobbing.

Chapter Twenty-nine

September 1812

It seemed all I did was plot. I spent every conscious moment thinking on how to bring Georgie around. I put as much effort into it as I'd put into beleaguering her before. And hating Walking Breeze. It kept me from thinking of Jemmy. And I was doing it for him, all at the same time.

Finally I came up with another plan. It took me a week to put it into action. I saw my chance on the eighth of September, at breakfast.

Grandfather was reading his mail. Aunt Hannah was pouring coffee out of her silver pot.

"Grandfather, I would ask a favor of you," I said.

"Well, ask. As long as it isn't about our trip to England. With this war, that is impossible."

Just then Uncle Richard burst through the front door. "General William Hull surrendered Fort Dearborn on August fifteenth," he said.

Aunt Hannah looked up. "Louis was at Fort Dearborn," she said.

Uncle Richard had a handbill. Everyone in

Salem knew by now that handbills boded no good.

"Surrendered?" Grandfather asked. "What of our army?"

"What army?" Uncle Richard sat down. "On the sixteenth, Hull surrendered Detroit, and the whole Northwest army without firing a single shot."

Grandfather was reading the handbill. "Massacre," he said. His hands were shaking.

"Massacre?" Aunt Hannah asked.

"Massacre." He said it again. "Indians attacked the Americans at Fort Dearborn and killed them all."

"Louis was at Fort Dearborn," Aunt Hannah repeated.

Grandfather threw the handbill on the floor. "This Hull is worse than St. Clair in the Revolution! Shameful, shameful!"

"Richard, what about Louis?" There was terror in Aunt Hannah's voice.

"I'm sure Louis wasn't there. We would have heard by now if harm had come to him," he said.

Color came back to her face. "But why did the Indians do this?"

From the corner of my eye I saw Walking Breeze coming from the kitchen with a plate of eggs and ham.

"Apparently," Uncle Richard explained, "there was an earthquake in December that lasted two days. The Indians considered it a sign."

"Louis told us of this sign," Aunt Hannah said. "The Indians were waiting for it."

"Well, since it came, Tecumseh had some small victories," Uncle Richard went on. "But big enough for General Brock to make Tecumseh a general in his British army."

Walking Breeze came into the dining room. No one took notice of her.

"Hull knew there would be attacks on his forts. So he ordered the evacuation of Dearborn," Uncle Richard said. "But the order came too late. The Indians attacked the fleeing whites."

"Damned Indians!" Grandfather swore. "They ought to be wiped out, every last one."

At that outburst, the platter Walking Breeze held crashed to the floor. And she ran from the room.

"Father!" Aunt Hannah chided, "see what you've done!"

"What I've done? It's what the damned Indians have done!"

Aunt Hannah went to see to Walking Breeze.

Grandfather turned his attention to me, scowling, remembering that I had asked him for something, spoiling for a fight. "Now, what did you want?"

"I wanted to ask if you'd let Georgie stop being a prisoner."

He looked at me as if I were demented. Not Uncle Richard, though. There was a light of encouragement in his eyes that kept me strong.

"How can you ask me such a thing now?" Grandfather growled. Then he picked up the handbill. "This is what Indians do when they are free."

Uncle Richard inclined his head at me. Ever so slightly.

"She's only half-Indian. But was raised white. And she was just trying to help, handing out the circulars."

"Help, is it?"

"Yessir. She was trying to do good."

"You're getting as meddlesome as your aunt. Sentiment will be whipped up to a frenzy now in town against the Indians."

"The Quakers know who she is and they accepted her in their meeting," I said.

"The Quakers are all crazy with their abstract notions."

"I met Samuel Morison at the Sun Tavern the other day," Uncle Richard said mildly. "He remarked that his wife said Georgie had become a respected member of their meeting."

"Did he now?" Grandfather sounded interested. Morison was a leading Quaker and a rich Salem merchant. "Still, he won't think so for long if she wanders the streets dressed as an Indian."

"She won't do that anymore, Grandfather. I promise."

"You *promise?*" This interested him for some reason. He leaned forward. "Are you willing to take her in hand and be responsible for her? Well, are you?"

I looked at Uncle Richard. Again he nodded slightly. "Yes," I said.

"I think this is something Ebie needs to do," Uncle Richard said with quiet authority.

Grandfather grunted. He picked at his fish and vegetables. "Very well," he said. "But the first time Georgie gets out of line, she gets confined again. Is that clear?"

I said yes. Across the table, Uncle Richard smiled at me.

Walking Breeze would not come out of her little lean-to room all day. She would not go to the mill.

Grandfather stood outside the door of her room. "Nancy!" He called her Nancy now. I suppose he thought that since she was doing such a wonderful job at the mill, she should have a white name, not an Indian one. "Nancy! The cloth you set in lavender yesterday has to be taken out of the tubs or it will be ruined!"

The door opened. She stood, tears streaking her face. "I cannot go with you. Tecumseh and my people fight with the king. I am now in the enemy camp!"

Grandfather's mouth fell open. "Great ghost of Caesar! What has that got to do with my lavender cloth?"

"You would wipe out my people!"

"They have wiped out mine!" he flung back at her.

"Then the council fire between us has gone out."

The door shut again.

"Nancy!" Grandfather yelled. "Only you know the right moment to take the lavender cloth out of the tubs! You worked so hard on it! All those elderberries and huckleberries you gathered! Nancy! I need you at the mill! Forget the massacre! Forget the king!"

But there was no reply from within.

Grandfather turned, looked at us, threw up his hands and walked out. "Do something with her, Hannah. I can't have this. I'm losing money."

"What can I do?" Aunt Hannah asked.

"Nothing." Uncle Richard stood there. "You have a wedding in a week, Hannah. But something should be done for Walking Breeze's sake. And this is the time when she will decide if she wants to be one of us or one of them."

He looked at me. "And she is going to need the protection of the family name if she is going to continue living in Salem. It's better she doesn't go out today. People know she is part Shawnee. In the mood they are in they could kill her."

Walking Breeze moved out of our house. She went to the boardinghouse where the mill girls lived. Two days before Aunt Hannah's wedding, Grandfather made an announcement at breakfast.

"If she doesn't come to the mill soon, I'll put her out of the boardinghouse. I'll send her away."

"Give her time, Father," Aunt Hannah appealed.

"I don't have time. I have orders to fill, cloth processed and ready for dyeing. The lavender cloth was ruined."

"That she spread her blanket at the boardinghouse is a good sign," Aunt Hannah said. "It means she still wants to be part of the mill. It's as if she's waiting."

He stared at her. *"Spread her blanket?"*

Aunt Hannah smiled. "It's a saying she has."

"And what, pray, is she waiting *for?"* he asked.

"I don't know," Aunt Hannah said. "She has promised to help at the wedding if she can stay in the galley on the *Prince.*"

Grandfather snorted. "It's about all she's good for," he said. "To help at a heathen wedding."

I said nothing. I had already set my plan in motion. If it didn't work, Aunt Hannah's wedding would be a disaster. If it did, my family might never speak to me again. Walking Breeze was waiting, yes. Despite what Grandfather had said to her, she was waiting. And only I knew what for.

Chapter Thirty

September 15, 1812

Early on the morning of Aunt Hannah's wedding, a sound pulled me out of my sleep. I was dreaming of Jemmy. It wasn't that I *saw* him in my dream as much as I *felt* his presence. And it was so real that I was annoyed when that persistent sound pulled me from him.

I sat up in bed. In the east, the sky was just turning from gray to purple. *Somebody was throwing something against my window.* I got out of bed, and went to look out.

Someone stood down there, waving at me.

It was *Georgie.*

No, I thought stupidly, *this isn't the plan. No.* And I pushed up the window sash. "What do you want?"

I could scarcely see her in the weak light. "I must talk to you," she said.

I hushed her and told her to wait right there. Then, with my heart pounding out of fear that she would wake the whole house and start Aunt Hannah's wedding day in an uproar, I threw on my robe and crept downstairs and outside.

"I don't want them to see me here." She was holding The Prophet, nuzzling him.

"What *is* it? Why did you come?"

She looked around, at the far reaches of the old house, as if it would attack her. "I came to tell you that my father is dead."

It was too early, surely, for this. And for a moment I thought she was playing one of her games to get out of her agreement with me.

But she was not. He was dead. Uncle Louis. She pulled a letter out of her pocket. It was travel-stained and wrinkled. It was from one of Uncle Louis's scouts.

I looked around. Everything was wet with dew. The world seemed wrapped in gauze, waiting to be opened. A new day. Aunt Hannah's wedding day.

I scanned the letter. "I can't read it," I said. "I just can't. Please, tell me what it says."

"He was killed in the massacre. The scout writes that because he was once adopted by the Indians, he knew he would be due special tortures when they took Fort Dearborn. So he blacked his face and hands and charged right into the fighting."

"Oh, Georgie," I said. I led her to a bench under the eaves of the house where we wouldn't be seen.

But there was still something missing. "Why didn't this scout write to Aunt Hannah or Uncle Richard?"

"He knew she was to be married. He instructed

his scout to send the letter to me, if anything happened. He didn't want to ruin her wedding day. The letter says I'm not to tell her until after she's wed."

The enormity of it swept over me. Uncle Louis, dead. No, certainly we could not tell this to Aunt Hannah. For a moment we sat in silence. All around us birds were just coming awake. The sky in the east was streaked with purple now. And some red.

"He was killed at once," Georgie said. "With one bullet."

"He was a good man," I said.

She stroked The Prophet. "I'm to tell her when I think the time is right. When do you think that will be?"

"Not until she comes home from her wedding trip," I said. "We must keep it a secret until then. From everyone."

We sat together, wrapped in silence. I couldn't become sensible of the fact that Uncle Louis wouldn't be coming home anymore. Even though he'd said that likely he'd not come east again, this was not what he'd meant, not what any of us had figured on. All my life, he'd been there in the background, part of Aunt Hannah's past.

"He loved her," she said.

"He loved you, too, Georgie."

"I don't know if I believe that right now."

"Why else do you think he sent the letter to you? He could have sent it to Uncle Lawrence."

She nodded. "He could have."

"You're his daughter. And he loved you. That's why."

She said nothing for a minute or two. "I don't know if I can do this thing today, Ebie," she said. There was a catch in her voice.

"Because of your father?"

"No, because I'm afraid. What if your grandfather gets angry? He'll put me away for a crazy."

"I won't let him. I'll take the blame if he gets angry." I leaned toward her. "It's the right thing to do. Uncle Richard said it. And Jemmy said it. And you know who else, Georgie?"

She shook her head, no.

"Your father."

Her eyes went wide. "He knew about the quilt?"

"No. But he knew about the broken days." And I told her of the conversation I'd had with him the day he left.

She nodded slowly. "I heard about broken days," she said, "when I was a child and went west."

"Then you see why you have to help me do this, don't you?"

"I'm still not sure, Ebie. I know it will help Walking Breeze. And it will help you. But what about me?"

I sighed. "I think you have some broken days, too, Georgie," I said. "And I think they're running out."

"Me?"

"Yes. Didn't you ever wonder? That mayhap it's time to forgive your father?"

She shook her head no. She moaned. She rocked back and forth. She hugged The Prophet. "Not fair of you to put it to me that way, Ebie," she said.

"I want to help you, Georgie."

"Why?"

I was still half-asleep. But I knew I must find the right words. "Because, when I was a little girl and my father first brought me to Aunt Hannah's, I missed my mother. So much, I wanted to die. But you played with me and read to me. You kept me from dying, Georgie."

"I did?"

"Yes. So I owe you, Georgie."

She brushed her hair off her face and looked at me. "Then why have you been treating me so bad?"

I felt tears in my throat. I reached out and patted The Prophet. He was purring. "I've thought on that," I said. "And I've decided it was because you went away. Because you went west. And when you came back, you were different. And I couldn't forgive you for it."

She nodded. I saw a new softness in her eyes.

"Everybody goes away from me, Georgie. They always have. My mother went away. My father goes to sea. So does Uncle Richard. I don't want people going away anymore. Not Walking Breeze. And not you, to any crazy house. I couldn't abide it. And so we've got to do this thing today. Don't you see?"

I commenced crying then. The tears started way down inside me, like something stored up for years. I started crying and I couldn't stop.

I don't know if it was for Uncle Louis. I'd never loved him. Most of the time he annoyed me, as a matter of fact. But I was hard put to stop.

In the end, she had to hold me to make me stop. It was then that I realized that her hair was washed and soft, and her dress was clean and starched.

"You've got your Quaker dress on," I said. "And your apron."

"Yes," she said. "Do you think it's all right if I wear this to do it in?"

Chapter Thirty-one

On the quarterdeck of the *Black Prince* I stood next to Mary as Parson Bentley said the words over Aunt Hannah and Uncle Richard. They both looked so handsome, I wanted to cry. I felt happiness swell inside me.

The sky was as blue as the silk dresses we bridesmaids wore. I closed my eyes and let the gentle lapping of the water against the *Prince*, the warm sun, and the parson's words seep into me. Aunt Hannah was getting married. Nothing else mattered.

Then I thought: *What if Georgie doesn't keep her part of the bargain? And everything is ruined for me.*

I looked at my grandfather, grave and stern, in his best broadcloth. Everything was ruined for him these days. The dyeing had come to a standstill at the mill, without Walking Breeze.

Aunt Mattie had tears in her eyes. My father stood with the Widow Berry next to him. Uncle Lawrence was looking solemn, but proud. And I wondered, what right did I have to mar the happiness of this day? Uncle Louis didn't mar it by dying.

Then I minded that I was doing what Uncle Louis would want, if he knew of it. And just then past all the bustle on the wharf, I saw Georgie coming.

I touched Mary's hand. She saw Georgie, too. Mary still couldn't believe what I had set into motion here.

Last night, as we'd decorated the *Prince* with flowers and streamers, I'd told her the whole story. Everything. From the way I'd first taken the quilt to how I'd tried to get it back.

Mary had listened, wide-eyed. Of course, she was taken with the drama of the whole thing. And she had promised to stand by me today, no matter what happened.

Now, as we became sensible of the fact that *Georgie was coming to Aunt Hannah's wedding*, Mary gripped my hand behind the silk folds of our dresses.

As the parson spoke of the responsibilities of marriage, Georgie came past Mr. Crowninshield's countinghouse. As he invoked the Lord's blessings on the couple, she came by Goodhue's Tavern. Then a notions shop. Then a bakery.

She came steadfastly, walking toward the *Prince*.

Just below us, she stood gazing up at the rigging. People moved around her on the wharf. Nobody knew her now as the crazy lady from the house at Twenty-one Union Street.

In her neat Quaker bonnet, apron, and cloak, with her wicker basket over her arm, she looked like any other respectable lady of Salem, out for an afternoon's shopping.

A sudden burst of joyous murmuring came from the crowd on the quarterdeck. The parson had finished with his words. Aunt Hannah and Uncle Richard were married!

Everyone crowded around them to take their hands and offer congratulations. Uncle Richard's crew gave out a cheer. Someone fired one of the *Prince*'s cannon.

Before the smoke cleared, Georgie was coming up the gangway.

As bridesmaids we had duties to perform. The guests had already had dinner, before the ceremony, served on long tables covered with white cloths. Now the cake and the wine would be served. It was our job, with the groomsmen, to hand out the cake.

Of a sudden, one by one, the babble of happy voices died out as people saw Georgie standing there.

Grandfather spoke first. "How dare you come here this day? You have been given orders not to wander alone through town!"

Georgie shrank back.

"Go to her," Mary whispered.

I ran across the polished deck and caught her arm just as she turned to go back down the gangway. "She's a guest." I stood holding her arm and facing my grandfather. "I invited her."

"You? By whose leave?"

"By yours," I said.

"Mine?"

"Yes." My heart was pounding. "You said I was responsible for her."

A distressed murmur went through the crowd.

Mary came to stand beside me. And for the awful moment that it took everyone to understand what was transpiring here, we stood our ground, the three of us.

Wrong, I thought dismally. *Why did I ever do this?*

Then Uncle Richard stepped forward. "Welcome, Georgie. Your aunt Hannah and I welcome you as a guest at our wedding."

Encouraged by his greeting, Georgie smiled. "I have come to see Hannah."

"Yes, Georgie, welcome," Aunt Hannah said. "My, you look fine."

"Do I look like a proper Quaker?" Georgie asked.

"Most proper," Aunt Hannah said.

"I have a gift for thee."

"A gift?" Aunt Hannah looked uncertain.

"Pray, Mary," I whispered.

"I'm praying," she whispered back.

By now all the wedding guests had their eyes fixed on the tableau we made. Some had now recognized Georgie. I heard one man whisper,

"Why, that's the half-Indian girl who's given the family such grief."

"No," someone else said.

"Yes. I'd know her anywhere. She's crazy as a loon."

"Poor Hannah," another lady murmured.

But all of this was nearly drowned out by the tremors and quakings inside me as Georgie reached into her wicker basket and drew out the gift.

We had wrapped it carefully, in paper from some tea chests from China. Georgie held it out for Aunt Hannah.

"Enough of this benighted nonsense!" Grandfather strode forward as if to stop Georgie.

"No," Uncle Richard said, "it's a wedding gift. Let her give it to Hannah."

Aunt Hannah untied the ribbon, opened the paper and stared at what was inside.

"It's a piece of old rag," Grandfather said. "An insult."

The guests were becoming uneasy. Some women looked alarmed.

"It's all right, everyone," Uncle Richard said. "Please go and get your cake and wine. We'll be over directly."

They dispersed. "I'll go help serve," Mary said.

I nodded weakly.

"I know it's not a proper gift," Georgie was saying, "but it's seemly. Lift it up and thou will see what it is."

Aunt Hannah lifted it, gingerly. At first she seemed dismayed. She did not recognize it.

And then she did. She gave a small cry. "Why this is a piece of my old quilt that I was working on! Long ago, with my sisters!"

Georgie was beaming and nodding her head vigorously.

"But it's changed!" Aunt Hannah said. And then she knew it for what it was. The knowing came over her like a great wave, taking her breath away. And she clutched the piece of quilt to her bosom. "Is it true, Georgie? And where did you get it?"

"Yes, it's true," Georgie said.

"Richard, do you know what this means?" Aunt Hannah clutched his coat sleeve.

His mouth twitched in a smile. "I know, love," he said. He hugged her close. Over her head, he smiled at me.

"But how, Richard? How?"

Thank God all the guests were crowded around the cake table. Only Grandfather, my father, Uncle Lawrence, Aunt Mattie, and Aunt Hannah were here to judge me.

"It came by mistake to my house in one of thy bundles," Georgie said.

I could have let it lay there, like that, between us. No one would have questioned it. Uncle Richard wouldn't give me away if Barbary pirates tied him to the mainmast of the *Prince*.

But there was a little problem I had to concern myself with.

I'd made myself a promise. No more secrets in this family. No more cages.

And no more broken days.

Oh, I had the secret of Uncle Louis's death weighing on me. But that was *his* doing, not mine. As soon as it was fitting and proper, I'd rid myself of that secret. *And then no more.*

So I spoke up.

My voice was shaky at first, but it gained strength from my sense of purpose. "No, that's not true," I said. "I put the quilt in the bundle and sent it to Georgie's house, Aunt Hannah. I wanted it to be lost and never found."

Grandfather responded first. "But you told me there was no quilt, Ebie. How do we come to this, now?"

How, indeed?

"I lied," I said. "I'm sorry, Grandfather."

"You *lied?*"

He could not believe it. He shook his head. He looked from my father to me to my father again. And of course, he knew where to lay blame.

"Now you see what kind of father you are," he told Father quietly. "Children learn from their parents. Do you have any idea what trouble this has caused all of us?"

Then he glared at me. For the true meaning of the matter finally settled on him. "Do you mean that Walking Breeze *is* my granddaughter, then? Is that what this means?"

"That's what it means, Grandfather," I said quietly.

"My God," I heard Uncle Lawrence murmur, "I knew it."

"Why did you lie to me?" Grandfather asked again.

Everyone was staring at me, waiting for me to answer. I saw the look of quiet encouragement in Uncle Richard's eyes.

"Because I wanted to be your only granddaughter," I said. "Because I wanted you to love only me."

"Why, I never heard such nonsense! Did you hear *that*, Cabot? You've raised a little liar. *Now* what have you to say to me?"

My father put his arm around my shoulder. "That you can't call her such," he said. "That my Ebie has done wrong, yes. But she owned up to it. And that you are partly to blame, Father."

"I? How so?"

"Because you couldn't love her," my father said. "Because you can't love anybody." He held me close. "I'm proud of Ebie this day," he said.

"Hear, hear," Uncle Lawrence said.

"That's right, coddle her," Grandfather said. "Make her more of a spoiled little piece than she already is. You've finished yourself with me, Ebie. There will be no trip to Europe now."

"Oh, I didn't mean to make all this trouble." Georgie was confused and agitated. "I must leave. Oh, Lawrence is looking at me. Oh, he's so stern."

"Stay, Georgie," Uncle Lawrence said. Then he turned to me. "Ebie, dear child." And he took me in his strong arms.

"You aren't angry with me?" I couldn't believe it.

"Angry? Of course not. Courage is shown in different ways, Ebie. If others don't always recognize it, that's their fault, not ours."

"It's all right about Europe, Ebie," my father was saying. "Don't worry. I'll take you to Europe."

"Should I leave?" Georgie whispered to me.

"No, stay at my wedding," Aunt Hannah said. "You are most welcome. Your gift is the best of all. And Ebie, oh, Ebie, I don't know whether to laugh or cry. So I'll just say thank you."

Of a sudden then, with all the hugging and tear shedding, someone minded that the person this was all about was not with us.

It was Uncle Lawrence. "Where *is* Walking Breeze?" he asked.

Everyone stood stock-still.

Grandfather, of course, played the role of hero. "I've sent a servant below. To fetch her. While all the rest of you are blubbering and making fools of yourselves."

We waited, nervously. In a moment Walking Breeze came up the companionway. She stood there, looking at us. Her apron was dirty, her hair coming in unkempt strands from under the neat cap, her sleeves rolled up to her elbows.

Grandfather took the piece of quilt from Aunt Hannah, walked over and handed it to her.

She smiled at it sadly, as one would at an old friend.

She wasn't overjoyed. I held my breath as her eyes set, first on one of us, then another. When those brown eyes came to rest on me, they stayed.

Grandfather was talking to her, rambling, in his low voice, as if the words were meant for her ears only. "So you see, you can help me at the mill now, can't you? I need your help. I can't do without it."

She walked right by him on the quarterdeck, not even paying him mind. He fell silent.

Very tall and straight she walked. Right to Aunt Hannah. Then she handed over the piece of quilt. "I give you this. From my mother to you," she said.

Aunt Hannah burst into tears all over again and hugged her. Then Walking Breeze turned to me.

I trembled beneath her look. I saw the amber lights in her eyes, the haughty lift of her head. Her stance seemed proud and ancient. I felt inferior and wanting. *She is going to strike me*, I thought.

Then, of a sudden, she smiled. "The time of the broken days is finished," she said. And she held out her hand to clasp mine.

Before I could answer, she turned to go back to the companionway.

It was my father who stopped her. "Walking Breeze."

She turned.

He reached out his hand. "Come join the family celebration. If you can forgive me. And all of us for what we have done to you."

She raised her chin in defiance. She looked again at us, one by one. My family returned the look, with nods and smiles.

"I shall always be Shawnee in my heart," she said.

"It's all right," my father said. "We could all use some Shawnee in this family. It might help us."

"And if I go back to the mill, it will be when my heart tells me to. And how my heart tells me to." She looked at Grandfather.

"As you please." He inclined his head in a little bow. "I will put you in charge of all the dyeing."

"Give me your apron, child," Aunt Mattie said.

Walking Breeze still hesitated. Then Aunt Mattie took off her silken shawl and placed it around her shoulders. "Now you are a guest," she said. She untied the apron and took it off.

"Should I stay?" Georgie whispered to me again.

I nodded. I had to nod, because I couldn't speak, for the stupid tears, as I watched them walking toward the table with the cake, Walking Breeze in their midst.

Epilogue

October 19, 1812

Dear Benjamin: I write, at long last, to thank you for your letter after Jemmy's death. I know it was meant to console, but I was not to be consoled at the time.

I beg your forbearance for the tardiness of my reply. I was grieving, and selfish in my grief. I thought it was mine alone. But Jemmy was your friend as much as he was mine. And I know how his death must have afflicted you.

I was remiss in not offering you condolences. But I always thought that men do not suffer the same as we women. It was Uncle Richard who told me they do. I do not know what I would do without Uncle Richard sometimes.

I know the Constitution now lies in Boston Harbor. Parson Bentley has a friend named John Carlton who has just been engaged as navigator. Parson Bentley says he is quite an able man.

What news can I give you of Salem? Uncle Richard and Aunt Hannah are married. He took the Prince out again on another cruise which is expected to last forty-five days, so he is not yet back. I live now with Aunt Hannah in their house and she and I enjoy many happy moments together. She says I am a most satisfactory companion. Yesterday we were invited to the gardens at John Derby's home and were given some nice apples and plums.

I'm still going to Mrs. Peabody's school. Mary and I joined the female singers at church. Our shipping is at a standstill because of the war. Parson Bentley says it may never recover and our port is in its declining years. Georgie has become a full-fledged member of the Quaker Meeting, and Walking Breeze has gone back to the mill, in charge of the dyeing room.

Oh, Benjamin, I write of everything but what is in front of my mind! I have treated you shabbily, and I fear you will be killed and I will never see you again.

When you last visited, I had eyes only for Jemmy. I minded how you stayed in the background and I wish you to know that I never meant to push you aside. You are, and always will be, my cherished friend. And I want you to come home from this war all of a piece and for us go again to Gallows Hill on the fifth of November and buy three-cent cakes on Election Day, and kiss in the stone tower on Winter Island.

Am I too bold? I think not. Once one has lost someone dear, one realizes how silly our conventions are.

But can we go back to those days when we were looking for the sea serpent? We both found him, didn't we? You in war and I by looking inside me, a place I never before dared go.

It was because of Jemmy, your gift to me, that I was forced to do such. He was better than Mary Wollstonecraft. And I will tell you all about it when we next meet. Which I hope will be soon. Come back to Salem, Benjamin, when you can. We will picnic on Winter Island. The sea serpent has gone. But perhaps the war will soon be over, and we can prove Parson Bentley wrong and watch the East Indiamen once again streaming out of the harbor.

Yr. affectionate friend, always, Ebie.

Author's Note

In writing this, the second book of my Quilt Trilogy, I decided to place the story during the War of 1812, not so much because this would be a story of war, but because this was the time of the second phase in the development of the cotton mills in New England. And the story of the Chelmsford family blooms and expands, as do the mills. And the country.

The first factory for the manufacturing of cotton cloth in this country was in Beverly, Massachusetts, in 1787, the time of the first book in the trilogy, *A Stitch in Time*. In this book, Nathaniel Chelmsford starts his mill in Beverly.

In 1814, the first power loom went into operation, in Waltham, Massachusetts, and this is the new factory that Ebie's grandfather, the same Nathaniel Chelmsford, is so excited about starting.

My reason for picking 1812 also has to do with the story of the Shawnee Indians. By 1809 Tecumseh was a name that commanded respect on the frontier. By 1810 tensions between Indians and whites were high in the Territory of Indiana where Tecumseh was a chief and William Henry Harrison Governor and Commander-in-Chief.

Tecumseh was attempting to unite all the Indian tribes in his "confederacy," and in July of 1811 he made a trip south to accomplish this.

In September of 1811, in Tecumseh's absence, his brother, "The Prophet" (whom I depicted as he was described in many accounts, vain, pompous, and stupid), was left in charge. And it was then that the warriors from the various tribes asked his permission to steal horses from white settlements. The Prophet gave permission. The horses were stolen, retrieved by the whites who came into the Shawnee camp, known as "Prophet's Town," then stolen back again by the Shawnee braves, luckily without any killing. But the incident had the potential for tragedy, since Harrison was waiting for exactly this kind of trouble for a reason to attack the Shawnees.

I used this incident to effect the trading off of Walking Breeze, by The Prophet, to keep the peace that could so easily have been broken. (Whites captured by Indians, or those who were half-white and half-Indian, were traded or "returned" all the time, when it was expedient for either party to make these exchanges. Many times whites did not want to go back to their own people, but were forced by politics or circumstances of the moment to do so.)

Walking Breeze is a fictitious character. However, the situation with the whites and the Indians on the frontier was adhered to with historical accuracy.

For the Shawnee vocabulary I am indebted to Allan W. Eckert. It was included in his wonderful book *The Frontiersmen.*

Since I now found myself in the era of 1812, I used the threat of the war in my story. It fell in wonderfully, with Richard Lander being away, captured by the British and thrown into Dartmoor Prison, where the British were just starting to put American seamen they impressed. Actually, throughout the war, many seamen were held there.

Tecumseh's background, his sister Star Watcher, his credibility as evinced in his awaited "sign," the earthquakes that came and were taken as that sign by the Indians, who then attacked, are all true. As is the attack on Fort Dearborn at the end of the book, in which Uncle Louis was killed, in August of 1812.

Louis Gaudineer, Hannah's star-crossed lover, is based on Indian Agent Captain William Wells, who had a dispute with Governor Harrison because Harrison was not paying the Miami Indians enough for the lands he was gobbling up from them. I have Louis, like Wells, preventing a massacre at Fort Wayne, being adopted by the Miamis, and then killed by Indians at Fort Dearborn.

Historically, American Brigadier General William Hull made a mess of the army in this war. He ordered the evacuation of Fort Dearborn and surrendered Detroit without a fight.

What other characters and events in this book are based on truth?

Well, Nathaniel Hathorne was seven and living in Salem exactly where I have him living. (He changed his name to Hawthorne only after he became a writer.) His mother was indeed a recluse; his ancestor was a judge in the Salem witch trials, and his people were cursed because of it. Another ancestor was a minuteman at Lexington.

There was a sea serpent haunting the waters around Salem and Marblehead at the time. He is mentioned in the wonderful *Diary of William Bentley, D.D.*, as are many of the other events in this book. It was by perusing this diary that I learned of life in Salem in these years, the feelings about the war, when commissions came through for the privateers, how so many seamen went to Dartmoor Prison, the various storms, the death of the descendant of John Proctor, the large glass bottle found with the name of Phillip English on it, the activities of the militia, and many other wonderful bits of information.

The sea serpent is New England folklore by now, also mentioned in *New England Legends and Folk Lore*, by Samuel Adams Drake. No one has ever explained what the serpent really was. But the people in Salem in 1812 really believed it to be a sea monster. They made every attempt to capture it, and Parson Bentley did report seeing it and wrote an account for the *Essex Register*.

The New England militia was, by 1811, the best in the country. And when President Madison called for troops from Massachusetts to take Montreal, Governor Caleb Strong refused the request. He sent only three companies of militia to the Canadian border.

I made Lawrence the commander of the Massachusetts State militia, a good role for him, since he became militant after Thankful was taken by the Indians. And, for the sake of story, I made Lawrence advise Governor Strong not to send the militia.

Privateers were the order of the day in the war of 1812, since our navy was not yet adequate. And many sailed out of Salem to "take prizes" and bring them back to port.

The War of 1812 was caused by Great Britain's impressment of American seamen. Some say it was brought on by America's desire to annex Canada. Others say it was the Indian unrest on the western border and the rise of Tecumseh, who was backed by the British.

Whatever was the cause, and likely it was all these three combined, it was considered the "second war for Independence." Nevertheless, the country was divided over whether to fight or not. In Salem the anti-British Republicans engaged in privateering against Britain. The Federalists seriously considered independence from the United States, rather than fight for "free trade and sailors rights." For such a cause was disastrous to foreign commerce and brought it to a virtual halt.

As for the other facts: The *Constitution* was anchored in Boston just at the time when Jemmy and Benjamin came to visit. And one of her most famous battles was with the British *Guerriere*, the fight in which Jemmy is killed.

The people of New England did keep Thanksgiving in the manner in which I have described. It was their big holiday, since they did not keep Christmas. And many of the festivities we enter into in our Christmas season, the parties and family get-togethers, were incorporated into their Thanksgiving. And, with the children dressing up and begging for treats, door-to-door, it seems as if they merged Halloween with it, as well.

Sarah Bryant, who is Aunt Hannah's friend in this book, really lived. By today's standards, she would be considered a "super-mom." She had seven children, five boys and two girls, born between 1793 and 1807. One of the boys was William Cullen Bryant, who practiced law, but later became a celebrated journalist and writer. Sarah kept house, wrote in a diary, made soap and candles, "spun a mop," whitewashed the walls, scoured the buttery, and wove cloth for the family clothing. As a young woman, she spun linen six days a week. After her husband died, she and her daughters were doing textile work on their New England farm, experimenting with color and design and exhibiting her wares at fairs. Eventually she brought in hired girls to do most of the work in her textile production.

I have her as a character, teaching young girls spinning, weaving, dyeing, and all the arts to do with textile production, because, to me, she represents the thousands of New Englanders whose home looms produced the textiles before the factories put them out of business.

And indeed, the underlying theme of the Quilt Trilogy is the birth and blossoming of the factory system in America, which started with the textile mills of Lowell, and which will be part of the third book of the trilogy, as viewed by Amanda, Abigail's granddaughter, and Jemmy's niece, who comes up to visit from St. Helena's Island in South Carolina.

Bibliography

Albion, Robert G., Baker, William A., and Labaree, Benjamin W. *New England and the Sea*. Mystic, Connecticut. Mystic Seaport Museum, Inc., The Marine Historical Association, 1972.

Coles, Harry L. *The War of 1812*. Chicago: The University of Chicago Press, 1965.

Eckert, Allan W. *The Frontiersmen*. New York, N.Y.: Bantam Books, 1970.

Eckert, Allan W. *Gateway to Empire*. New York, N.Y.: Bantam Books, 1984.

Hawkins, Robert. *The Kent Family Chronicles Encyclopedia*. New York, N.Y.: Bantam Books, 1979.

Hawthorne, Hildegarde. *Romantic Rebel, The Story of Nathaniel Hathorne*. New York, N.Y.: Appleton, Century, Crofts, 1932.

Heckewelder, Rev. John. *History, Manners and Customs of The Indian Nations Who Once Inhabited Pennsylvania and the Neighbouring States*. Philadelphia: The Historical Society of Pennsylvania, 1876.

Horsman, Reginald. "The Paradox of Dartmoor Prison." New York, N.Y.: *American Heritage*, the Magazine of History, Vol. XXVI, No. 2. February 1975.

Mahon, John K. *History of the Militia and the National Guard*. New York, N.Y.: Macmillan Publishing Company, 1983.

Miller, Edwin. *Salem Is My Dwelling Place*. Iowa City, Iowa: University of Iowa Press, 1991.

Nylander, Jane C. *Our Own Snug Fireside, Images of the New England Home, 1760–1860*. New York, N.Y.: Alfred A. Knopf, 1993.

Salem, Maritime Salem in the Age of Sail, Washington, D.C., U.S. Department of the Interior, Produced by the National Park Service, Division of Publications: 1987.

Smith, Peter. *The Diary of William Bentley, D.D. Pastor of the East Church, Salem, Massachusetts*, Vol. 4, January 1811–December 1819. Gloucester, Mass.: Peter Smith, 1962.

Stuart, Reginald C. *War and American Thought, From the Revolution to the Monroe Doctrine*. Kent, Ohio: The Kent State University Press, 1982.

Tharp, Louise Hall. *The Peabody Sisters of Salem*. Boston, Mass.: Little Brown & Company, 1988.

Viola, Herman J. *After Columbus: The Smithsonian Chronicle of the North American Indians*, Washington, D.C.: Smithsonian Institution, Distributed by Orion Books, a Division of Crown Publishers, 1990.

Weisberger, Bernard A. *"The Working Ladies of Lowell."* New York, N.Y.: *American Heritage*, the Magazine of History, Vol. XII, No. 2. February 1961.

Welles, Arnold. *Father of Our Factory System*. New York, N.Y.: *American Heritage*, the Magazine of History, Vol. IX, No. 3. April 1958.

About the Author

ANN RINALDI is one of today's best-known writers of historical fiction for young adults. She is the author of six ALA Best Books for Young Adults, including *In My Father's House* and *Wolf by the Ears*, winner of the 1994 Pacific Northwest Library Association Young Reader's Choice Award, Senior Division, and one of the 100 "Best of the Best" ALA Best Books for Young Adults of the last 25 years. Ms. Rinaldi is also the recipient of an award from the DAR for her historical fiction.

Ann Rinaldi lives in Somerville, New Jersey, with her husband.

point

Other books you will enjoy, about real kids like you!